Rolo's
STORY

DOG'S
EYE
VIEW

For Killian, Finn, and Zoe

tiger tales
5 River Road, Suite 128, Wilton, CT 06897
Published in the United States 2021
Originally published in Great Britain 2020
by the Little Tiger Group
Text copyright © 2020 Stripes Publishing Limited
Illustrations copyright © 2020 David Dean
ISBN-13: 978-1-68010-255-0
ISBN-10: 1-68010-255-9
Printed in China
STP/1800/0425/1021
All rights reserved
10 9 8 7 6 5 4 3 2 1

www.tigertalesbooks.com

Rolo's STORY

DOG'S EYE VIEW

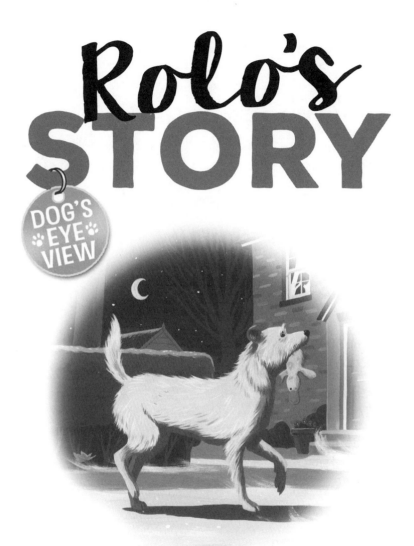

by BLAKE MORGAN

tiger tales

Contents

Chapter One
A Free Dog

Sniff, sniff, sniff. My nose twitched like crazy as it picked up the scent: warm and meaty and delicious. *Sniff, sniff.* Dog food? *Sniff, sniff.* A juicy bone? *Sniff, sniff.* No, even better—steak!

My claws tapped on the kitchen floor as I closed in on my target, only to find that the food was high above me on the kitchen counter where my paws couldn't reach.

That steak really does smell good, I thought.

Although I'd prefer it served in a bowl on the floor. Maybe with a side of bacon. But I'll take what I can get.

I scrambled onto a dining chair, rose up on my hind legs, and clawed with my front paws at the kitchen counter. *I. Just. Can't. Reach.*

A-ha—I know! I bounced up and down on the padded chair—*boing, boing, boing*—I was getting closer! After a few bounces, I managed to pull myself onto the counter. But just as I was about to sink my teeth in, the plate rocked off the edge and landed on the floor with a loud *clang!*

All of a sudden, an angry voice shouted, "Mutt! Is that you, Mutt?" A tall, dark shape appeared from behind the kitchen door. It was one of those mean, furless creatures. A Two Leg. My owner.

A shiver of fear ran through me, right to the tip of my tail. My legs started to tremble, and my heart was beating so loudly that I could hear it in my ears. I leaped off the kitchen counter and turned to run—the steak now forgotten. My owner ran after me, chasing me out of the kitchen and into the yard.

"It's no use running away from me!" he shouted in his booming voice. "I'll catch you, you rotten dog!"

He was getting closer and closer, and when I turned to look and saw the rope he held in his hands, I almost tripped over my paws. My whole body trembled with fear. He was going to tie me up and leave me outside in the yard again. It was so cold and lonely out there—I couldn't bear the thought of it. Even a life as a stray would be better than that!

He was just reaching out to grab me when—

I woke up with a jolt. My legs were

twitching frantically, as if I were still running. My dream had felt so real … because it *was* real. It had all happened, just like that, on the day I finally ran away. Except for the steak—that really had been just a dream.

My nightmare brought it all back—how my owner would leave me on my own for days at a time, forget to feed me, shout at me when I'd done nothing wrong, tie me up outside during the cold winter nights. I might only be a mongrel mutt, but no dog deserves to be treated that way. That's why I decided to stand on my own four paws— to make it by myself in the world—to run away and live *rrruff*. How hard could it be?

That evening, almost a week since I'd left, I was outside, sheltering under a tree from the biting cold. "*Ow-ow-owww!*" The wind howled and I howled back, trying to scare it away. The moon looked like a pale gray ball just sitting there in the sky, as though waiting to be pounced on. It gave off a murky light that helped me to see in the darkness.

I was in a strange new place after traveling all day. *A patch of dry grass, some rusty old swings, railings all the way around ... must be a park*, I thought. Even though I was in unfamiliar territory, it was much too late to go any farther, so I'd have to stay here for the night and get some sleep. As I lay down under a bench, my ears twitched at the sounds of unknown creatures rustling in the trees and bushes. I felt more alone than ever.

Grrrowl! That wasn't me—that was my stomach. I was so, so hungry. I hadn't eaten in ... I don't know how long it had been, but it felt like many dog years. If only I knew my way around the park, then I could have hunted for some greasy food wrappers to lick. *Yum!*

As I thought about food, the hunger pains kept tugging at my insides, and I let out a wail. "*Ow-howl!*" But what was the use? Nobody was going to hear me, and even if they did, they wouldn't care. You just can't trust a Two Leg. At best they let you down, and at worst, they're as cruel as cats. I had to be my own master now. I had to keep going and never look back. I might have been suffering from the hunger and the cold, but it takes more than that to keep this dog down!

I lifted my nose. A soft breeze had blown a strong smell of—*sniff* —trees, then something more promising—*sniff, sniff*—maybe something good to eat — *sniff, sniff*—something like—*sniff, sniff*—FRUIT!

The smell reminded me of the only time I'd ever eaten fruit. I was trotting down the main street with my old owner on one of the few times he took me out for walks. We got to a shop with fruit and vegetables on a stand outside. As we passed by, a plum rolled off onto the pavement, and I gobbled it up before my owner could stop me— stone and all!

Now, I could smell the sticky-juicy-yumminess of plum once more. I followed the scent across the grass. It was as though I were on a leash—an invisible one that was pulling me toward the delicious fruit. I trotted along eagerly, my tail wagging with excitement.

There it was! A huge tree towered in front of me with a whole heap of plums scattered underneath. I gazed happily at the fruit. *You're mine, all mine!*

I scampered over to the tree, my tongue

hanging out and dribble running down my furry chin. I'd almost reached the fruit when a frightening noise made me freeze.

"*KRA! KRAAA!*"

From high in the tree's branches, a flock of ravens flew out into the sky. They moved as one, like a pack of foxes, making my ears ache with their sharp screeching. "*KRA! KRAAA!*"

I can't speak a word of Raven, so I couldn't understand a thing they were saying. But I did know this—they were heading straight for my fruit! The biggest one swooped down on the nearest plum and tore off a mouthful. I started to edge forward slowly, carefully, to make my own claim, but the bird whipped its head around so I was level with its pointy beak. I was only a young puppy, but I'd been around long enough to know that I shouldn't fight something with a beak sharper than my teeth!

When the biggest raven was full, the rest of the flock landed and started pecking the fruit to pieces. The large bird watched over them, making a *caw-caw-caw!* noise that sounded like it was laughing at me. Then all of the other ravens finished eating and flew up into the sky. And all that was left behind was a pulpy mess of skin and stone.

So that was it. No food for me. The only thing I could do was find somewhere to curl up and get some sleep. *Maybe I shouldn't have run away—at least I had food and shelter when I lived with my old owner*, I thought miserably. Most days I'd get a few scraps to eat, like cold rice or pasta left over from his dinner. Okay, so sometimes he'd completely forget to feed me, but at least I didn't starve.

No—I had to stop thinking like that. I couldn't just sit around feeling sorry for myself. I left home because I was unhappy there. If I just kept my tail up and carried on, I'd be much better off on my own. I trotted over to one of the benches—one with a pile of dried leaves underneath. I turned in a circle three times to carve out a nest for myself, and then flopped down heavily and rested my head on a paw.

I knew I'd feel better after a dog nap. Maybe tomorrow I'd find something even yummier than a plum. This thought cheered me up and got my tail wag-wag-wagging again. That's right—I was a free dog. Free to do whatever I liked, however I liked, whenever I liked …. I just hoped there'd be some food involved!

Chapter Two
The Long, Long Ears

The next morning, I stayed snoozing on the pile of leaves while the sun was high in the sky. When it hid behind the horizon again, I headed out. It was safer to move under the cover of darkness when there was no chance of a Two Leg spotting me.

I walked down street after street. House, house, driveway, house, house, house, lawn. I *really* wanted to roll around in the grass and feel its velvety touch against my fur, but I knew it was too risky to get that close to where the Two Legs lived.

Every now and then I could smell a dog inside one of the houses: the horrible, clean stench of a pet dog that's just had a bath. *Yuck!* Ever since I went *rrruff,* I'd become a big fan of dirt. But as bad as the clean dogs smelled, each time I picked up their scent, I couldn't help picturing them curled up on a soft couch, all safe and warm in front of a crackling fire. I imagined them being patted on their heads and thrown juicy bites from their owners' dinner plates. And for a moment, I wished I was one of those indoor dogs.

But then I saw a garbage can next to a window where—*sniff*—I could smell—*sniff, sniff*—bacon inside! Although it was raw and probably old, garbage can bacon was way better than any Two Leg food.

Next to the garbage can, there was a length of short wall, so I rose up on my hind legs and hooked my front paws over the edge, hoisting myself up until I could clamber onto the can with a *thunk!* I cringed at the sudden noise and jumped as the front door of the house creaked open and an unmistakable shape appeared. A Two Leg, alerted by the sound. I desperately wanted to dive into the garbage can and find the bacon I'd worked so hard for, but there just wasn't time—the Two Leg would get to me before I got to the bacon. *Come on—quick! Run for it while you still can!*

I ran and ran until I reached the end of the street, where I turned the corner to find stores everywhere, with bright lights glaring onto the pavement. I darted past a few until I came to one selling—*sniff, sniff*—food. When I saw what was waiting outside, my heart started to thump in my chest. It was a sausage dog tied to some railings by a leash. It was stuck there! What if the dog had been tied up by a Two Leg and left there forever? The thought brought back memories of being tied to the pole in my owner's backyard. My legs started to tremble, but I couldn't just stand by and watch. I had to do something!

I crept over to the sausage dog and introduced myself with a few quiet woofs. "Hello there. My name's Mutt, and I'd really like to help you."

"Mutt? What a funny name!"

I couldn't understand why the dog was smiling when she was so clearly in danger. "Are you okay? I can see you're tied up to that railing. Who did this to you?"

"It was my owner, silly! He just went inside to pick up takeout."

I knew it! I knew it was the dirty work of a Two Leg. And not just any Two Leg — the poor dog's *owner* had done this to her!

"*Grrr.* Typical. My owner used to tie me

up all the time, too—I hated it. But don't worry—I'm going to set you free!"

"Set me free? What are you talking about? I'm waiting here for my owner."

"You mean … you *want* to be tied up like this?"

"Of course! I like my owner. It's nice having someone to give me my dinner and take me on walks."

"So … you're not a dachshund in distress?"

"I'm only in distress because you're pestering me."

"Don't you want to escape your leash and run free? I'm a runaway stray, and I've never felt happier!"

Before she could reply, my ears pricked up at the sound of a tinkling bell. The shop door was opening, and I could smell the awful scent of a Two Leg approaching. I took one last look at the dog, just to be sure she was okay, and then I made a quick getaway before the Two Leg spotted me and tied me to the railing, too.

I kept going until I found myself in what seemed like an even busier part of town.

The cars on the road were making loud vrooming noises and I closed my eyes, feeling safer if I couldn't see what was happening. But the sounds got louder with my eyes closed, and I whined quietly because my ears were hurting and I felt like I was in danger and needed to hide.

Come on, now—you have to be brave, I told myself. *You can do this! Just put one paw in front of the other.*

Slowly, my paws began pounding the pavement again, and I flattened my ears to block out the sounds of the cars zooming past.

Pant, pant, keep going....

I swerved around a flashing light from a passing car.

Pant, pant, just a little farther....

I dodged another bright beam.

Pant, pant, almost there....

Finally, I slowed down as I reached some tall metal railings, which I was small enough to squeeze under. I emerged on the other side on a long, gray platform. But before I could decide where to go from there, I heard a voice coming from farther down the platform. I whipped my head around and saw a Two Leg sitting on a bench.

"Hey there, dog!" the Two Leg shouted.

My tail moved nervously from side to side, and I let out a big, frightened yawn.

"What you doing here all on your own, feller? Why ain't you with your owner?" Although the Two Leg spoke with a soft, trembly voice, I was still scared that it would catch me and return me to my old owner. I watched it closely as it reached for a long, wooden stick that was resting against the bench and stood up slowly. "Come here, feller. Let's get a good look at you. Where's your collar?"

The Two Leg walked jerkily toward me, holding its stick in one hand and flapping the other in the air. "Come on! Come here, boy!"

I usually love sticks, but this one looked suspiciously long. *What if the Two Leg hits me with the stick?* My old owner used to wave an umbrella at me, threatening to hit me with it. He never actually did—but the threat hurt almost as much as the real thing. The memory left me frozen in panic. *Should I stay still, or should I run? I could growl fiercely and snap my teeth to scare the Two Leg off. But what if that doesn't work?*

My thoughts were interrupted by a strange honking noise. As the sound grew louder, a strong wind ruffled my fur. The Two Leg looked down the platform to where a huge train was pulling into the station. And while it was distracted, I saw my chance, turning on my paw pads and darting off in the other direction.

When I finally stopped running, my legs were trembling. I just about managed to drag myself into some nearby bushes. When I was far enough inside to be hidden from sight, I licked my fur nervously to comfort myself. *Phew—that was close!*

Eventually, once everything was still and silent, I felt brave enough to creep outside again. I lifted my nose to investigate my new surroundings. *Sniff, sniff.* A wild creature had been there—I could tell because it had left fresh markings all around. What if it came back, whatever it was? But before I had a chance to make any kind of plan, a nearby bush started to rustle. Then that bush stopped and a closer one rustled, followed by an even closer one. Someone, or something, was spying on me!

Rustle, rustle, rustle.

I started to weigh my options. *If it's a creature looking for a fight, I should probably run away. I'm not very good at fighting....*

Before I had another moment to think, a furry thing rolled out of the bush and gave a growl that made me shiver. That is, until I really looked at the animal and realized, *Phew—it's just another dog!*

Maybe she's alone like me, I thought. *Maybe we can help each other!* I wagged my tail hopefully, my tongue hanging out to one side.

"*Bark, bark!* Hello! My name is Mutt."

"Hello, Mutt. I'm … um … well, nobody's ever given me a name. But the squirrels around here call me Scrap the

Squirrel Snatcher, so that's what I tend to go by. But you can just call me Scrap." I could see why the squirrels called her that. Scrap certainly looked scruffy. Her fur was so long and matted, it looked like she'd never been groomed in her life. But then, I couldn't talk—after only a week of living *rrruff,* I was hardly looking like a show dog myself.

Scrap seemed to be a mongrel like me, but with her large eyes and long, long ears, I guessed she also had a trace of beagle in her. She moved—carefully and slowly—toward my neck, raised her nose—which was marked with what looked like cat scratches— took a long sniff, and … jumped back and winced.

"What's that on your neck?" she cried.

"Oh, this?" I said, bowing my head with embarrassment. "It's a scar from a rope. My owner used to tie me up with it."

"That sounds painful! But then again, what d'you expect when you're somebody's pet?"

"Hey—who are you calling a pet?" I asked, offended. "I used to be, but not anymore. I'm my own master now. My old owner was horrible to me—he'd leave me alone all day and never once petted me.... That's why I ran away."

"Good for you! Welcome to the Four Seasons Hotel! Looks like you haven't been enjoying your stay too much—I can see your ribs right through your fur. Haven't you found the self-service buffet yet?"

"Oh, no—I don't go into restaurants! It's too scary. What if a Two Leg sees me?"

"I'm only kidding! What I mean is—haven't you been eating leftovers from the garbage cans?"

"Oh! Well, I've tried, I really have, but I keep getting caught."

Scrap shook her long, floppy ears and made some tutting noises. "Sounds like you've got a lot to learn. But the good news is, you're in luck. You've just met the number one guide to life on the wild side!"

Chapter Three
Playtime

The next day, Scrap and I went to find some breakfast at the local park. As she led me to a nearby garbage can, her experienced paws hardly made a sound on the pavement. With a *yelp* she launched straight into the air, landing soundlessly on the edge of the can with the balance of a squirrel on a fence. She pried open the lid with her paw, reached in with the other one, dug out a half-eaten burger, and dropped it into my paws. Then Scrap dug out another for herself and jumped down to join me for a delicious, greasy snack.

While we were filling our bellies, I had a great idea.

"Hey, Scrap—why don't we play a game?"

"I don't play games, Mutt. Not if they won't fill me up or keep me warm. You need to remember that it's tough out here—we can't waste any precious time or energy."

"Please?" I begged. "Nobody's ever played with me. Well, except for when I used to grab my owner's slippers in my mouth—then he'd chase after me for a while. But I don't think that was a game, because he'd yell and shake his fists at me."

"I'm no expert on Two-Leg behavior, but that definitely sounds more angry than playful to me," Scrap said between mouthfuls of her burger. "I really am sorry, Mutt, but there's too much to do today, like finding water to drink, shelter to sleep in.... And besides, I've never played any games before, so I wouldn't know where to begin."

"That's okay—I can teach you!" I said, sensing a small chance to persuade her. "If you use your imagination, you can turn anything into fun! My owner never gave me much to play with, so I used whatever I could get my paws on: a dried leaf, a pigeon feather, an empty water bottle."

Scrap looked kindly at me. "Well, maybe you could just show me how—"

I was so excited at the idea of playing with my new friend that I let out the biggest, loudest *YELP!*

"*Shhh!*" said Scrap urgently. "Stop making such a racket, Mutt. Someone might hear you. You don't want to draw attention to yourself. You've heard the rumors about the dog pound, haven't you?" Her fur bristled with fear.

"The dog pound?"

"Yeah—it's a prison for dogs where Two Legs lock you up for the rest of your life. You never see the sky or step on the grass ever again. Imagine!"

I shuddered all over.

"It's okay. They're not going to get you—I'll make sure of that. You just need to keep your yelps down, that's all." Her gaze softened. "Look, if you promise not to make too much noise, I'll play a quick game with you. Deal?"

"Deal!" I answered, wagging my tail. "Ooh—I know! There's a game that my owner played with me once when he first got me. I think it's called Fetch, because he kept saying fetch, and I kept having to fetch." The day we played that game, it only lasted a little while. My owner seemed to get bored really quickly. But this time, Scrap and I played Fetch together for a long time.

First, I raced around the park until I found an amazing stick—have I ever mentioned how much I LOVE sticks?—and then I paused and bounced up and down. Scrap watched and waited, wriggling her bottom. She stared eagerly at the stick, like a hungry dog gazing longingly at a juicy steak. Then, with my mouth, I hurled the stick into the air.

Scrap chased after it, tail waving in the wind, paws hardly touching the ground, running faster and faster until she seized the stick in her teeth. But she didn't quite understand what to do after that.

"*Bark, bark!* Bring it back to me! Over here, Scrap!"

She stared at me with a doubtful look in her big eyes. Then she dropped the stick at her paws, looking confused.

"Why did you throw it away if you wanted

to keep it?" Leaving the stick where it was, she danced over to me empty-mouthed. When she reached me, she let out a high-pitched *yelp*. "You know, this is pretty fun. I never knew how exciting a stick could be!"

"*Bark, bark!* Scrap, you're supposed to *fetch* the stick!"

"Huh?" she answered, getting more and more confused by the rules of the game.

"I have an idea—let's switch!" This time, I picked up a stick in my teeth and passed it gently to Scrap to throw for me.

I raced across the grass, far away from her, eyes wide, tail wagging, mouth open, tongue flapping. Then I stopped and gave an encouraging *bark*. Scrap tipped her head to one side, not understanding what she needed to do. Then she bounded across the grass toward me, the stick still in her mouth.

"Throw the stick! Throw the stick!" I

called. But Scrap wasn't going to give up her new toy that easily.

I tried and tried, but finally, I gave up and slumped down into a tired but happy heap on the grass. *Pant, pant, pant*…. It felt so good to have a playmate. Even if she was terrible at Fetch!

As the weeks passed by, Scrap stayed loyally by my side, and I by hers. She was so clever and always seemed to know what to do, so I stopped worrying about how I was going to find food and where I was going to sleep. I even stopped worrying about getting caught by a dreaded Two Leg. I felt bouncy and full of energy again, as if I could run around and play all day.

I never knew why Scrap was alone like me—why she didn't have any family or other friends. I tried to ask her if she'd ever had an owner, but she always changed the subject. Maybe she had a horrible owner like mine once and was just too upset to talk about it.

One evening, it was Scrap's turn to go foraging in the garbage cans for dinner. She gently placed a paw on my paw to say good-bye, like she always did. And then she scampered off toward the big road up the hill with all the cars.

As the night wore on and Scrap didn't return, a strange feeling began to grow in my tummy, like that sickly feeling I get when I eat grass. I tried to keep myself busy by grooming my fur, but I couldn't help thinking that something wasn't right. Scrap was taking too long. What had happened to her?

When the sun began to rise over the rooftops and she still wasn't back, I knew for sure that something was seriously wrong.

I searched everywhere—the garbage cans where we'd scavenge, the park where we'd play, the canal where we'd bathe. I was about to head home to the bushes we slept in, just in case she was waiting for me there, when I picked up a scent. It was faint, but it was definitely Scrap ... mixed with the unmistakable tang of fear.

I sped toward the smell faster than a greyhound after a rabbit. I ran beyond our usual territory and found myself lost in a crowd of trees and brambles, dark and uncontrolled. But although I didn't know where I was, I never lost track of Scrap's scent. It got stronger and stronger until I made my way out of the woods and reached a street busy with cars. In that moment, I didn't care about the speeding vehicles blocking my way—I just had to get across the street to Scrap. I knew

I must be close now—I could hear her cries on the wind.

"I'm here! Don't worry! I'm coming for you, Scrap!" I ran toward her voice, darting across the street and skidding around the corner. Then I saw it: a big, gray van with a huge cage on the back. And inside the cage, looking out at me with terrified eyes, was Scrap.

"They got me, Mutt! They're taking me to the pound!" Cooped up inside, she looked so afraid. "I outran them for a while, all over town, but I just couldn't shake them."

I edged toward Scrap, desperate to break her free. "No! Don't try to stop them—you might get caught, too. Just take care of yourself, Mutt. Good-bye!"

"No, no, no! I'll save you, Scrap! They can't take you away from me!" I howled, but the van was already starting to drive away. I ran as fast as I could, my legs struggling to keep up with the huge rolling wheels. A thick cloud of gray smoke pumped out of the exhaust pipe, choking me and misting up my eyes so I couldn't see a thing, and I was forced to tumble to a sudden stop.

With tears welling in my eyes, I desperately looked up and down the street. No van. No Scrap. It was just me ... all alone again.

Chapter Four
Beak Face

Scrap was gone, and I was filled with a terrible sense of loss. I had to bite down hard to hold back the whimper of sadness that was wanting to burst from me. If only I could have saved my friend!

As time went by in a blur of lonely nights and lonelier days, the only thing that kept me going was Scrap's favorite saying, which she loved to repeat to me, especially when times were hard: "Life is tough, but so are you."

But while Scrap had taught me a lot about survival, she disappeared before she could teach me how to cope in the storms and snow that came with winter. When I first ran away all those months ago, the wild had been an easier place, filled with gentle breezes, bright flowers, and fruitful trees—but things had changed. The fruit and flowers had shriveled up, and now the winds howled through the parks, making the trees, and me, tremble.

One morning, as the gray clouds hung in the sky, I made up my mind—I needed to move on. I had to find somewhere with warmth and food—somewhere that didn't remind me of Scrap. I was going to search for a new home, and I'd keep going until I found one. You see, dogs like me never give up. Not then. Not now. Not ever.

I took a big, deep sniff of the early

morning air. *Today smells of ... hope. Who knows—maybe I'll finally manage to catch my own tail!*

As I left my bushy home for the last time, I caught the scent of some garbage cans just a bone's throw away. My new home could wait another few minutes while I had a good-bye meal, right?

I found a garbage can that wasn't too tall and nudged the lid open with my paw. Lying at the top of the trash, poking out of a plastic bag, there was a stuffed toy—a furry duck with a big beak and only one eye. Forgetting about my rumbling tummy, I grabbed the beak in my front teeth and jumped down onto the pavement.

My very own toy! I'd never had one before. Well, I did have a sock once that I stole from my owner, but the stuffed duck was way better than a holey old sock! I dropped it at my paws to get a better look. The poor thing was all scruffy and abandoned. It stared at me sadly with its one big eye as if to say, "Nobody loves me. Will you be my friend?"

I buried my nose in its fur. *Sniff, sniff, sniff.* It had a wonderful smell of the garbage can—all fishy and cheesy and yummy. *What should I call my new stuffed friend? Let's see … it has a big beak … on its face…. I know! Beak Face!* I wagged my tail with satisfaction at my excellent choice of a name. A warm, loving feeling washed over me—the first one since I'd last seen Scrap.

By the end of the day, my body was aching with cold and hunger. I'd traveled so far, through parks and woods and fields—I'd even swum across a river—but I wasn't getting anywhere fast. So, I decided to take a risk—to go into a nearby town to try to find food and shelter.

Beak Face and I trotted along in silence until we came to a large house. There was something about it that felt safe and welcoming. In the front yard, there were neatly clipped bushes, ivy growing up the walls, and pots of bright pansies that were somehow surviving the winter cold. And down the side of the house, I could see a gravel path leading to a neat backyard. I was so tired that I couldn't resist the idea of a warm bed for the night—even if it was on a Two Leg's territory.

I crept across the frosty lawn to where there was an old garden shed. *What was it Scrap taught me about opening shed doors?* I rose up on my hind legs and flung myself at the door lock. It took a few tries, but finally the stubborn thing broke. Then I pawed the door open and snuck in cautiously.

Inside, the wooden floor was covered with a lot of clutter. And above was a roof with small cracks through which you could see the stars in the sky. It was hardly a luxury dog spa, but it would give enough shelter to get me through the night. So, I dropped Beak Face on the floor, curled myself around him, and fell asleep in two shakes of a dog's tail.

"*Ow-owww!*" I awoke with a start. *Where am I? And why is everything so dark?* I thought in sleepy confusion. *Oh, yes, the shed!*

I scratched the sleep from my half-closed eyes with a back paw, stretched my legs one by one, and rolled over onto my side, enjoying the luxury of being indoors for once. In the distance, I could hear a faint sizzling noise that sounded like bacon frying in a pan. I licked my lips at the thought.

A loud voice snapped me out of my daydream. "Freya, hurry up and get your skateboard! Your breakfast is almost ready!" It sounded like a Two Leg, which would usually send me bolting in the opposite direction, but I was hungry—and where there are Two Legs, there's FOOD.

I forced myself up off the cold wooden floorboards and turned to my new friend. "How are we going to steal that Two Leg's food without getting caught?"

Beak Face stared at me blankly with his one eye.

Before I had time to think up a plan, I heard some noises coming from outside, closer than the voice. It sounded like something—or someone—was heading toward the shed. As the door creaked open, I backed away in fear, all my courage gone in an instant, and crouched down low, making myself as small as possible.

A figure filled the door frame. *A Two Leg!* I wanted to turn and run, but it had already seen me. There was nowhere to hide.

"What? How on Earth did you get in here?!"

Chapter Five
Freya

"Hey! Look at you. You must be the cutest thing I've ever seen!" The Two Leg was talking in a strange kind of voice that I'd never heard before—high and calm and sweet. *What's it up to? I don't trust it. Oh, no—it's crouching down onto its knees! And its hand is coming straight toward me!*

At the sudden movement, I felt a heaviness low down in my tummy, then a warm, wet sensation between my legs. I couldn't help it. I looked up shakily at the

Two Leg, terrified it would shout at me.

"Oh, you poor thing! Did you go to the bathroom on the floor? Please don't be scared—I didn't mean to scare you." It started to lean in toward me, moving slowly.

I growled a warning: "*Grrr!*"

"Don't worry, I'm not going to hurt you. Oof—you smell a little, don't you? But then, I bet I smell pretty funny to you, too!" The hand moved slowly toward me again, and my whole body started to tense. The hand quickly drew back, and I relaxed. *That's a good Two Leg!* I thought.

There was something very odd about its behavior—it hadn't shouted at me or shooed me away, like most Two Legs did. Maybe it was scared of me—I must have looked pretty tough after all that time on the run. I barked to let it know just how tough I was. "*Bark, bark, bark!*"

"It's okay, it's okay. Oh!—" The Two

Leg raised a hand to its mouth in shock as it caught sight of the scar around my neck. "What's that? Are you injured? Did somebody hurt you?"

Strange. I'd expected the Two Leg to be disgusted, but it just sounded concerned. I still didn't trust it, but my doggy instincts told me I might be able to use it to get food. I had to take the chance, in any case....

"*Woof, woof, woof!*" *I'm so hungry. Please feed me. Please!*

"That's it—someone *did* hurt you, didn't they? What a horrible person!"

"*Woof, woof!*" *No, no—I want you to give me something to eat!*

"Yes, yes—that's right! I'm going to make it better. I'm going to bring you some healing cream for your neck."

"*Bark, bark!*" *No, no! You've got it all wrong. I don't want healing cream—I want food! You know, like a slice of ham or some peanut butter, or even just a greasy potato chip bag?*

"Oh, I wish you could understand what I'm telling you," the Two Leg said. "Then you'd know I'm trying to help you—that I'm your friend."

The word made me pause. I'd never had a Two Leg as a friend before. Hmm— time to sniff it out and see if it really could be trusted. It smelled female and slightly of— *sniff, sniff*—bacon. *I think maybe I could be friends with this girl....*

Another thing that made me think she was okay was that she had a tail like me— except hers was on the top of her head and tied up with a ribbon!

The Two Leg made a face that looked happy as I sniffed around her knees. "Aw, you're adorable, aren't you?"

My ears started prickling and twitching, but not from her praise—someone was shouting outside. "Freya! Freya! Your breakfast is ready! Come and eat it before it gets cold!"

Freya. That must be the young Two Leg's name.

"Oh, no—it's Mom! Quick, quick—she's coming!" Freya jumped up and started flapping her arms around, looking really excited.

A-ha! I know what this means—Freya wants to play! I beat my tail against the hard wooden floor and panted in short, sharp bursts with my tongue hanging out. I *love* playtime!

Freya looked around quickly. Her head jerked left and right, up and down. *Hey —I get it! She's looking for something to throw!* I bounded over to the other end of the shed and paused, vibrating with excitement, waiting for Freya to find a stick or a ball. *Oh, please let it be a ball! I love balls even more than sticks!*

"What's taking you so long, Freya? You're going to be late for school!" came the voice from outside again, even closer this time.

Freya crouched down next to me and said softly in my ear, "You have to keep quiet—please!"

Ooh ... she must be getting ready to throw something! I couldn't help but let out a big, excited *BARK!*

"*Shhh!*" Freya hissed. Then she rushed out of the shed, shutting the door with a slam behind her.

What just happened? Where did she go? I thought we were going to play a game.... I slumped to the floor in disappointment. *I knew you should never trust a Two Leg. Just when you think they're being nice to you, they go and let you down again.*

Outside the shed, the rain started to pour. I could hear the droplets on the roof going *plip plop plip plop*. It might have been lonely in the shed, but at least it was dry. Best to stay for a little longer until the rain went away.

I stayed in the shed for what seemed like forever when suddenly, Freya opened the door again, letting in a cold draft. This time, she was carrying a big cardboard box, which she placed on the floor. "Here you go, doggy. You can sleep in here tonight. I know it's not much, but it's better than the cold floor—trust me."

I gave the box a good sniff and noticed a soft blanket had been folded inside it. Freya tapped the box with a hand and said in her high-pitched voice, "Bed!"

But I didn't really want to sleep in the dark, dank shed for another night. Not now that I knew there was bacon inside the house. So I did sad-doggy-eyes at Freya, hoping she'd take pity on me. *Let me sleep in your warm house. It's so cold in here—I'll freeze. Pleeease?*

"I'm sorry, little doggy, but you'll have to stay here tonight. I can't let Mom see you. She's super strict, and there's no way she'll let me keep a puppy."

I whined pitifully.

"You see, Mom likes to have everything organized. She makes schedules for chores and sets alarms on her phone, like for when we need to turn off the TV. It bothers her when things interrupt her routine. So having an animal in the house would make her head explode! I've asked her for a pet so many times, but she always says no. Although she did give in once. I asked for a rabbit for Christmas … so she, um, bought me a stick insect. Same thing, right?"

Then something odd happened—Freya

made a noise that sounded like laughter. I never knew that Two Legs could laugh! My old owner certainly never did. I pricked up an ear and listened carefully to see if she'd do it again.

"The stick insect literally did nothing except sit on a branch all day—it didn't even change position—but Mom found it to be the most stressful thing ever. She'd say that I wasn't feeding it, or cleaning the tank, or checking that it was still alive— even though I was doing *all* of those things! Then one day, the stress obviously got to be too much, and while I was at school, Mom took the tank from my room and tipped it into a bush in our backyard. It might have been the most boring pet ever, but I loved that stick insect!"

Freya fiddled with the metal thing on her wrist. "Oh, no. It's getting late. I should really get back inside—Mom will be wondering where I am." She rose from her knees, where she'd been curled up next to me. "Night night—sleep tight. Tomorrow's Saturday, but I promise I'll get up super early to come and see you before Mom wakes up." And with that, she vanished through the door.

Typical Two Leg! She abandoned me again! But it was too late and cold outside to find anywhere else to sleep. I was feeling really sorry for myself now—it was so dark in the shed, and the rain was starting to drip through the roof and land on my fur.

My thoughts drifted to when I lived with my old owner. When it was bedtime, he'd either shut the bedroom door on me and make me sleep on the hard hallway floor, or he would drag me into the yard and tie me to a post. The cold, lonely nights seemed like they'd never end. And I'd go half crazy worrying that my owner would never come back for me.

Now, I paced back and forth, fear and hunger building up inside me. Then I had an idea. Even though Freya had left me for a second time, I could tell she was nothing like my old owner. She seemed kind and caring, and best of all, she smelled like bacon. She wouldn't want to leave me outside all night.

"Watch this!" I said to Beak Face.

I started to whimper softly. When that didn't work, I turned up the volume to a whine. Still no response. So, I decided on a full-on howl. I put everything I had into it—enough to melt the heart of even the cruelest Two Leg. "*OW-HOOOWL!*"

A distant noise sounded from the house: a door opening and closing. My plan had worked. I held my breath and waited until the shed door swung open and Freya reappeared.

You came back for me! I knew you would!
I quivered with joy and wagged my tail
frantically. Then I bounced around Freya's
feet while she made a laughing noise that
sounded like chirping birds.

Freya reached out to pick me up off the
floor. As her hands got closer, my thoughts
sped up with last-minute doubt. *Can I
definitely trust this Two Leg? What if she
puts me somewhere even worse than this leaky
shed? But if she can be trusted, she might take
me inside her warm house, and there might
even be food....*

I decided to take the risk and let Freya put
a warm hand around my shivering belly. As
she scooped me off the floor and lifted me
to her chest, I grabbed Beak Face in my
teeth—I'd never leave him behind! Then
Freya picked up the bed-box in her other
hand and whispered to me, "I could hear
you howling all the way from the kitchen,

doggy. I felt so sorry for you!" And with that, we stepped out into the night.

When we reached the back door to the house, my heart pounded—a mix of nerves and relief. As Freya opened the door, there was a loud creak. I felt her take in a sharp gasp of breath. I held my breath, too—after all, I didn't want anyone to catch us now that we were so close to food and proper shelter.

We continued on through a kitchen, down a hallway, and up a long, carpeted staircase. Step. Step. *Creeeak!* Step. Step. Then....

"The box!" whispered Freya as the cardboard slipped from her hand and fell down the stairs with a loud *thunk*!

From upstairs, a sleepy kind of groaning sounded in response.

Freya left the box and bounded up the rest of the stairs like a startled rabbit, me and Beak Face still cradled in her arms. At last we'd arrived at our destination: the bedroom.

"Look—we made it, puppy! Having a secret dog is way more exciting than having a stick insect!"

This is more like it—a bright, warm, dry bedroom! I thought to myself as I took in my new surroundings. It had been so long since I'd felt soft carpet beneath my paws!

Freya disappeared through the door and came back a few seconds later with the bed-box. She placed it down next to me. "There you go, doggy."

I picked up Beak Face and jumped in gratefully, turned around in a few circles, and curled up. In that dreamlike moment, I felt as though a golden light was glowing inside my tummy. I was just so happy to be warm and dry once more.

Chapter Six
Mom

Early the next morning, before it was light, Freya popped her head over my box. "Morning, doggy!" she said with a big smile on her face. "I hardly slept at all last night—I was so excited! How about you? Did you sleep well? I think you probably did— you were making funny snoring noises all night!" She laughed her chirpy, birdy laugh.

"You're so cute, aren't you? What were you doing in the shed all alone?

Where's your owner?"

I whimpered and did sad-doggy-eyes at her to beg for food.

Freya looked at me sympathetically with her big brown eyes and seemed to understand exactly what I was thinking. "Hey, I almost forgot—you haven't had any breakfast. You must be getting really hungry. You stay where you are, doggy, and I'll see what I can find downstairs. Just don't make a sound—Mom can't find out that you're here!" Freya sprang up, startling me, and then she disappeared through the bedroom door.

Soon, I could smell a delicious scent coming from under the door. *Sniff*—it smelled like—*sniff, sniff*—turkey! I wagged my tail so hard that it *thwacked* against the side of the box. Then I danced around and let out a big, excited *YELP!*

Seconds later, Freya burst through the

door and came running toward me, waving her hands. "*Shhh! Shhh!* Mom will hear you!"

Quick as anything, she dropped some slices of meat in front of me. *Yummy, yummy, turkey in my tummy!* I gobbled them up in a few gulps and licked my lips all the way to my whiskers. Then I licked the blanket where the turkey had dropped, just to make sure I didn't miss anything.

"You have to be quiet now. That's a good puppy." I'd heard the word "quiet" before. It meant I should keep my mouth shut or I might get a smack on my nose. But I'd never heard a Two Leg say "good puppy" before.

Before I could think about what it meant, a voice shouted from outside the bedroom door. "Freya! Do you have your guitar book? You have a lesson today, remember."

"Um … yes … I'll get it now." Freya looked around the room in a panic.

"Are you okay, Freya?"

"Yes, Mom. I'm, um, fine. Everything's fine."

Then the doorknob started to turn as the Two Leg tried to open the door.

"I have the guitar book, Mom. No—don't come in! *Stop!*"

Suddenly, everything went dark. It looked like some blue fabric had landed on top of my box.

"Are you sure you're okay, Freya? You sound a little strange. Are you nervous about your guitar exam?"

"Um…."

"Don't worry—a few nerves are good for you. They should motivate you to keep on practicing. And then you'll be able to get through those tricky scales, won't you?"

Everything is so dark in this box! I feel so

trapped! I started to whine with fear. "*Ow, ow, owww!*"

"Freya—what's that noise?"

"What noise, Mom? I don't hear anything."

I don't like being in this box anymore. How do I get out? Which way is out? "*Ruff, ruff, ruff!*"

"There it was again, Freya!"

"It's nothing, Mom! It must be coming from outside."

I have to get out! I'm really scared! I started to scratch frantically at the cardboard with my claws.

"Freya—what's going on? What do you have down there? What's moving under that robe?"

"*Ruff, ruff, ruff!*"

"Please, Mom! Don't touch that!" A shadow loomed over my box.

"*Ruff, ruff, ruff!*"

"No, Mom! Stop!"

"*Ruff, ruff, ruff!*"

"Freya! Where on *Earth* did you get this *dog*?!"

At first, I thought the bigger Two Leg's name was "But Mom!" After all, that's what Freya kept saying to her in a high, whiny voice. But after a while I realized she was just "Mom."

When Mom had recovered from the shock of finding me hiding in Freya's bedroom, she sat Freya down at the kitchen table, me at her feet, and gave her a stern talking-to. "Okay, I've booked an appointment at the vet for Thursday. That's the earliest they can see him, unfortunately."

What's a vet? I wondered.

"But Mom!" Freya's voice sounded stressed. "He doesn't need to go to the vet—he just needs a bath! We can give him one on our own. It's really easy—I helped Zoe from school bathe her sheepdog when I was over at her—"

"Freya—it's not about him being dirty. We can't just take in a strange dog—he might already have an owner," Mom said. "I know he doesn't have a collar on, but we need to take him to the vet to see if he's microchipped. His owner might be worried sick about him!"

Not likely, I thought.

"But you're always saying how you wish I had more company," Freya said. "And now that I have a puppy to play with, you're trying to take him away from me!"

I could smell the tension coming off both Two Legs. I didn't understand what they were getting so worked up about. They were all warm and dry in a house filled with turkey slices. They had it easy.

"It's for his own good, Freya. Anyway,

he'll have to stay here for a few days before the vet can see him. So you'll get to spend time with him when you get home from school. That'll be nice, won't—"

The Two Leg was interrupted by a noise—a *bring-brrring* sound coming from her jacket pocket. It made me jump and scrunch my eyes shut. I didn't like Mom's noisy pocket one bit—it had been going off all morning.

"I'm sorry, Freya, but I'm going to have to take this call. It's my boss." And with that, she rushed out of the kitchen.

Phew—she's gone! I opened my eyes again and looked up at Freya.

"Mom is always working. Work is more important than everything else—even on weekends. It's so frustrating!" Freya was frowning. "I'm always asking if we can do something fun or go somewhere new, but she just says she has to finish some work thing first. And by the time she's free, it's always too late to do anything. But today should be different—it's not like we get dogs wandering into our yard every day!

"What if you don't even have an owner? What if you could stay here and be my little puppy? I'd love that—I'd love it so much!" She smiled down at me, but then her frown came back again.

My little puppy. The words confused me. I knew what they meant all right, and sure, I was starting to like Freya. I just didn't know what to think about being some Two Leg's pet again.

Chapter Seven
Rolo

After I'd been living in the house for a few days, I knew that when the darkness transformed into bright light, it meant my breakfast was ready. *Wag wag wag!* I'd eaten as much in the past days as in the whole time I lived on the streets. The house was cozy and warm, too. Twice a day, the huge cream radiators under the windows filled with heat, and warmth rippled through every room.

I couldn't have dreamed everything, could I? Would I wake up any moment and nothing would be there anymore? Maybe I was just imagining warm radiators, glowing lampshades, bowls full of food and water. I'd be back on the streets—back to the hunger, the cold, the cruel ravens, the endless rain…. But it was only ever the freezing streets that vanished like a bad dream.

Not everything was perfect in the house, though. For starters, there were some very strange noises that I'd never heard before. Every morning, ringing sounds went off upstairs. (I later learned these are called "alarms.") They were so loud that they made me tremble. As soon as the Two Legs heard them, they'd instantly obey the noise and come rushing out of their bedrooms like very well-trained dogs. Then there were all the sounds from the Two Legs' breakfast: the *whistling, sizzling, clattering, slurping, clinking*. I liked these because they usually meant Freya would throw me some yummy pieces. But the loudest noises of the day were the leaving-the-house ones. These always ended with Mom shouting, "Hurry up, Freya! You're going to be late!"

For the past few days, Freya had disappeared from the house for a long time—and I'd started to miss her when she did. Even though I had my stuffed friend, Beak Face, I couldn't help feeling a little lonely without her.

Freya told me she went to a place called school. From what she said, I gathered this was where Two Legs trap you in a room, tell you what to do, and hardly let you see the sky or step on the grass.... Sounds a lot like the dog pound to me! But Freya also told me that you get to learn amazing things at school ... like why the sky is blue and how birds hunt for worms. Apparently, they stamp on the grass, which makes the worms think it's raining and lures them to the surface. Yum—I might try that one day!

When Freya got back from school each day, I'd follow her around because she was the Giver of Good Things: a rubber ball, a small piece of cheese, a blanket under the radiator, a fluffy slipper.... Okay, so she didn't give me the slipper—I took it from her bedroom when she wasn't looking— but I think it still counts.

Unlike Freya, Mom stayed at home in the daytime, tapping away on a gray box on the table. I really wasn't sure about her—I was finding her much harder to trust than Freya. I was convinced she had her eye on my beloved Beak Face because one morning, when Mom, Freya, and I were in the kitchen, she started to stare at my stuffed friend oddly. She had a look of disgust on her face—the way I look when it's time for my bath....

"Freya, what's this stuffed duck thing? Do you know where it came from? It's disgustingly dirty—I think I'm going to have to throw it in the garbage." Mom started to move her hand toward Beak Face.

"*Grrr! Ruff, ruff, ruff!*"

"Mom, don't! Please!" Freya jumped up at my growling. "He loves that stuffed duck. Can't we just put it in the washing machine?"

"But it's so dirty that I'm not sure that'll be enough."

"We can try, though, can't we? Please? I'll do some extra guitar practice!"

"Well, okay. But I don't want you to just practice the easy scales."

"Ugh! All right. It's a deal."

As Mom finally moved away from Beak Face, I threw my paws around him and held him close to my fur. *Phew!* My stuffed friend was safe ... for the moment.

I headed over to the huge glass door that separated me from the yard. Outside, I could see the shed. I was glad I didn't have to sleep in there anymore. But oh, I wished I could go out and roll around in all the wonderful grass. I'd been inside for what felt like forever and was starting to get itchy paws.

I let out a howl of longing, which Mom interrupted. "Freya—why is the dog making that noise? I hope he's not going to pee all over the floor again—I just mopped it yesterday."

If I could, I would've blushed. I didn't mean to pee on the kitchen floor. And anyway, I don't know what Mom was complaining about—the floor smelled a whole lot better once I'd finished with it!

"I think he just wants to go out. I'll take him for a run around in the yard...." Freya moved toward the door, and I rocked back on my hind legs, eager to stretch them.

"Hang on! You need to get your stuff ready for school!"

"Can't I play with the dog quickly first? Please, Mom? If I tire him out now, he'll be less likely to bother you while you work."

Mom looked thoughtful for a moment. "Okay. But don't be too long."

I gave a hopeful *yelp* and jumped up at Freya's leg. She patted me on the head and opened the kitchen door.

Ah! Fresh air!

And I was off—ears flapping, paws thumping the ground, tongue flopping out the side of my mouth—it felt *great*!

Freya and I raced around the yard together until I just couldn't go on. I slumped down into a satisfied, panting heap and started rolling around in the grass, twisting and turning on my back. Freya flopped down and rolled around, too. *Oh, yes, this Two*

Leg isn't like the others, I can tell. This one is different. Then suddenly, I felt compelled to do something that I vowed never to do again for as long as I lived.

I poked out my little tongue and…

I licked the Two Leg's hand.

Later that evening, Freya and I cuddled up on her bed surrounded by mounds of bedding and hills of soft, downy pillows. I loved Freya's bedroom. If I ever felt scared or unsafe, it had a lot of good hiding places, like under the bed, behind the wardrobe, or inside the hamper.

Freya turned to me. Her soft yellow tail fell over her shoulder, and her big brown eyes gazed at me curiously.

"I wish I knew your name, little one. How about … Fido?"

"*Bark!*" *Too boring.*

"Snowy?"

"*Bark!*" *Too wintry.*

"Max!"

"*Bark!*" *Too Two Leggy.*

"Lucky?"

"*Bark!*" *Too untrue.*

"Sir Barkalot?"

"*Bark!*" *Now that's just silly.* I had much better ideas than Freya. Doglins the Dog! Woofo the Wild! Wagtail the Wanderer! Proudpaw the Pup! Barko the Brave!

But Freya kept calling out more silly names: "Pip! Toby! Buster!"

At this rate, Mutt sounds pretty good to me, I thought gloomily.

"Ooh, I know! What about Rolo?" Freya looked down at me with a huge grin. "Rolo! Come here, Rolo!"

I suppose it did have a certain ring to it.

"Rolo!"

And Barko the Brave probably wouldn't fit on a dog collar anyway. Well, Rolo it was, then! A new name for a new start! I gave a loud *yip* of approval.

"That's the one!" Freya clapped her hands together—she seemed very excited that she'd finally thought of a decent name. She patted her lap, and I rewarded her by crawling onto it. "Mom says I shouldn't give you a name because I'll get too attached. But I can't just call you 'doggy' all the time, can I, Rolo?"

Freya burrowed her fingers into my fur, which made me feel all tingly. "You know what else I've been thinking about, Rolo? I've been wondering what kind of breed you are." She gently moved me from her knee and jumped up. "Wait here while I get Mom's laptop."

Freya left the room and returned a moment later with the strange gray box

Mom used during the daytime. She sprang back onto the bed and balanced it on a pillow in her lap. "Look, here's a rescue dog website—this might help."

She gazed at the screen with a thoughtful expression.

"Now let's see…. Wiry, sandy-colored coat? Check! Round black nose? Check! Pointy ears? Check! Brown eyes? Check! It sounds like you might be a terrier-cross. Thank goodness you're not a cross terrier, though—that wouldn't be good, would it, Rolo?"

Ha! The Two Leg made a joke. I didn't know they could do that!

Freya ran her hand along my back, and I closed my eyes contentedly. I was starting to get used to her fussing over me.

"It's got a list here of common terrier-cross traits…." She nodded thoughtfully. "Yes, you *are* energetic and playful! And you *do* like to chase me around! Ooh, it says you can be loyal and loving, too. Awww! But also naughty and troublesome. Well, Mom might agree with that, but I think you're an angel!"

I rolled over onto my back and waggled my paws in the air to show her I was cute as well as angelic. Freya giggled and then turned back to the screen. After scrolling for a while, she started to look a little worried. "The site says stray dogs can be frightened and reluctant to trust humans. Poor Rolo! You're not scared of me, are you? You know you can trust me, don't you?"

I nudged my nose into Freya's hand, hoping to signal that of course I knew that now.

"Oh, I wish you could be my puppy forever! That would be amazing, wouldn't it?" Although that sounded pretty good to me, Freya sighed and looked upset.

Don't worry, Freya—I know how to cheer you up! I jumped down off the bed and sniffed my way to a pile of shoes on the floor. I chose a shiny brown one that smelled like new leather. I picked it up in my teeth, jumped onto the bed, and dropped it next to Freya to signal the start of playtime. I knew how to get a party started!

Freya laughed. "Oh, Rolo! That's my new school shoe!" She reached her hand out for the shoe….

Oh, no, you don't! You'll have to chase me for it! I leaped off the bed and darted to the other end of the room. On my way, I tripped over a rug—whoops!—and did a big somersault with the shoe still in my teeth. Then I chomped down on the shiny leather and shook the shoe crazily from side to side, daring Freya to take it from me.

She held her stomach as it jiggled up and down with laughter. I bounced around her feet and dashed past her grasping arms. *Pant, pant, pant—this is so much fun!*

Freya crept forward slowly and was just within reaching distance when Mom called from outside the room: "Freya—what's all that stomping around? You should be in bed by now."

"But Mom, it's only eight thirty."

"Yes, I know. But you need to be up early tomorrow because we have the vet appointment. Remember?"

Freya's face fell. And when she didn't reply, the bedroom door opened, and Mom's feet appeared, followed by the rest of her. "Freya! What is the dog doing in here? You know he's not allowed in your bedroom!"

"Oh, I'm sorry, Mom. It's just that he was scratching at the door, and I felt really sorry for him. And anyway, Rolo—"

"Who's Rolo?"

"Um, nobody."

Mom bent down and started to inspect the chewed-up shoe that had fallen out of my mouth. *Ooh, I bet she's impressed with how I've improved it—how I've covered it with slobber and managed to rip off that ugly buckle!*

"What's this, Freya? What happened to your new school shoe?" Mom's voice was quickly getting higher and louder. I started to cower and crept slowly under the bed. "Look, Freya, it's ruined! And where is the buckle? I just bought you these!" I flattened my ears and lowered my head.

"It was that dog, wasn't it, Freya?"

"No, Mom, it was me…."

"I know it was the dog. He's obviously guilty—look how he's hiding under the bed. And the shoe has bite marks all over it. He completely destroyed it!"

"Stop shouting, Mom. Please! You're

scaring him." Freya crouched down to talk to me. "It's okay, little one. There's nothing to be scared of. The big noise will stop soon."

But Mom continued. "I've had it up to here with that dog. He's out of control!"

"He didn't mean it! He's just a puppy!" Now Freya's voice was starting to get loud, too.

"He's a menace! He chews everything, he makes messes everywhere, he keeps us up at night...."

Hey—what's wrong with chewing, making messes, and barking? I poked my head out from under the bed in sudden outrage.

"But he makes things fun around here!" Freya shouted, and I darted back into my hiding place. "Oh, I forgot—that's not allowed."

"Freya, stop being so rude! That dog is a bad influence on you."

"*Howl!*" *Hey—that's not fair!*

"It's just as well that he's going to the vet tomorrow. Hopefully, they'll be able to find his owner."

"No, Mom! Please!"

"Freya—this isn't a debate. He has to go, and that's that."

I looked up at Freya's face, where tears were starting to shine on her cheeks. She looked so sad that it made me feel hurt, too—like a splinter of glass was stuck in my paw.

As the tears rolled down her face, Freya whimpered, "Please, Mom. You can't take Rolo away from me. He's my best friend."

Chapter Eight
The Journey

The next morning, Mom placed a box on the kitchen floor by the oven. It looked as though it was made of plastic, and it had a metal grille on the front, like a kind of door. I'd never seen it before and would have given it a big investigative sniff, but I was quickly distracted by a delicious slice of turkey that Mom had taken out of the fridge. *Ooh—a treat! Maybe Mom is finally warming up to my irresistible doggy charms!*

Mom started to creep across the kitchen

toward me, waving the turkey in front of her. I bounded forward to meet her and followed the turkey right into the plastic box....

Clang! The metal door shut firmly behind me.

She tricked me! I'm trapped! Help! As I howled my head off for Freya to come and rescue me, Mom carried me and the box out of the house and to the car. It was dark and cramped inside, and the metal bars reminded me of the cage Scrap was trapped in when she was taken away. *Maybe that's what the vet is—just another name for the pound.... Help! Let-me-out-let-me-out-let-me-out!*

Freya was already waiting inside the car in the back seat. As Mom placed the box down next to her, she whispered through the bars in a choked-up voice, "I'm so sorry, Rolo—there's nothing I can do."

As the car zoomed along, Freya didn't say a word to Mom, but I growled and howled until my throat was raw, even though I knew it was no use. How could Mom be doing this to me? I closed my eyes tightly and started to tremble. It felt like there was a balloon inside my chest getting bigger and bigger, making me pant for breath.

Suddenly, Mom's voice made me jump. "Freya, what's that smell?"

"I don't know what you mean."

"It smells like it's coming from where you're sitting. Will you take a look?"

Freya's face appeared at my door again. "Oh, no, Rolo peed himself! But don't scold him, Mom. He's shaking with fear back here—he obviously couldn't help it."

Help—Mom is going to be so angry with me now!

"Oh, Ro-lo!" But she sounded more tired than anything. "Freya, can you just hold on to the pet carrier for me so it doesn't spill out? We'll be there any minute."

The car finally stopped, and Mom jumped out. She carried me through a glass door into a room that smelled too clean and made my head spin. I was just about to start howling when I heard a strange voice.

"Hi there! I'm Lisa—the vet you spoke to on the phone." This Two Leg had a really horrible smell, too—like flowery soap and clothes that had just been washed. *Yuck!*

It unlocked the door of the box, and I backed away from the door until my bottom hit the other side of the box.

What does this smelly Two Leg want? Better try to scare it off. I bared my teeth and made as much noise as I could.

Freya bent down and cooed into the box, "*Shhh!* It's okay, Rolo. Just calm down."

But I was too scared to calm down. And before I could come up with an escape plan, the Two Leg reached inside, scooped me out, and put me on a long table. Then it picked up a pocket-sized machine, which it waved across my shoulders and along my back.

"He doesn't seem to be microchipped. There aren't any contact details showing up on my scanner at all. So I think it's fair to conclude that this poor little fellow doesn't belong to anyone."

Mom let out a sigh. Freya let out a squeal of excitement.

The Two Leg continued, "Since he doesn't have an owner to claim responsibility for him, I'm afraid I'll have to send him to the local animal rescue—"

"Woof?!" What's that?!

"Mom, we can't do that to him!" cried Freya.

"Unless, of course, you'd like to adopt him," said the Two Leg.

"Please, Mom, please! There's nothing in the world that would make me happier!"

Mom paused for what felt like days. She looked up at Freya, and then down at me. Then she said, "Oh, Freya. Okay. If he really means that much to you, I guess we'll have to keep him."

When we got home from the vet after dropping Freya off at school, I was so grateful to Mom for letting me out of the box that I completely forgot she was the one who locked me in there in the first place! I squirmed my way onto the couch where Mom was sitting and nuzzled into her lap.

"Rolo, the vet told us earlier that you don't have an owner."

Well, I did have an owner once....

"And I've been thinking that that's just not fair, is it? Every dog should have a family who loves him."

I don't think my old owner ever loved me.

"You might be naughty and steal all my socks … but Freya loves you so much already, and I suppose she's right—you do bring a certain amount of fun into the house. It's strange—all this reminds me of the dog I had when I was a child. My parents adopted poor Misty from a rescue center, and I fell in love with her instantly. It was lucky for her they did, too—all dogs deserve a home of their own." Mom smiled down at me. "So … this is your home now, Rolo."

"*Hooowl!*" I was so happy that I bounced along the couch and fell right off it. Thank goodness my bottom has fur padding!

That evening, Freya was completely transformed. Before we went to the vet, she'd been moping around the house, bursting into tears and arguing with Mom at every opportunity. But the moment she got home from school, she was full of excitement, like a toy mouse that's been wound up tightly and suddenly let loose. And I was every bit as excited as she was! My whole body quivered from all the wonderful feelings that were bubbling up inside me.

At bedtime, as usual, Freya snuck me into her bedroom. Even though Mom was allowing me to stay, she still had rules.

"I can't believe Mom agreed to let me keep you! She's always so strict."

Tell me about it! She never lets me eat any of her pens and pencils.

"Even if it's a Saturday and I want to sleep in, Mom says I have to get up, and she pulls the covers off me."

Or if it's pouring rain and I want to roll around in all the muddy puddles in the yard, she won't let me outside until every drop of rain has stopped.

"I'm actually a good kid. If Mom saw how naughty some of the other kids at school are, she'd be thankful to have me."

I know, I know! I flicked my ears to show I was listening. *If only we could train Mom to be less serious. Maybe teach her some new tricks.*

"Anyway, I just can't believe Mom is letting you stay! At first, she seemed like she'd never give in. Even when I said that having a pet would help me become more responsible, she didn't budge. I wonder what on Earth could've changed her mind...."

I know what it was, I thought to myself. *I wonder if she's ever told Freya about her beloved Misty.*

Freya was gazing out of the bedroom window with a faraway look on her face, so I nudged my wet nose into her hand to get her attention again. "You're a funny puppy, Rolo!" she said, rubbing my snout and giggling. "Oh! I almost forgot. After school, I bought you a present to make up for this morning. I think you'll really like it!"

Freya slid off her bed and fumbled in her school bag. When she returned, she had a harness of some kind in her hands. It was made of soft-looking fabric decorated with blue and white stripes. She held the harness to my nose so I could have a good sniff. "You're part of the family now, Rolo."

It took me some time to get used to my harness. At first, I absolutely hated it when

Freya tried to coax me into it. I put my tail between my legs and scurried into the bathroom, where I tried to pull it off against a basket. The next time, I zoomed right under the couch as soon as I caught sight of it in Freya's hand. But then, when she wanted to go out for a walk another day, Freya tried something different.

She started by placing the harness on the floor in front of me, and every time I even looked at it, she laid down one of my absolute favorite dog treats. I love them so much that I start wanting one even when I'm eating one. They're a little taste of doggy heaven—a bit of dried beef, followed by subtle hints of sawdust and sock drawer. They're the best!

While I was busy scarfing down my treats, Freya gently lifted my front paws and placed them in the harness loops. At the same time, she kept filling my mouth with more treats. I couldn't even *bark* to say thank you! And before I knew it, I was all strapped in and ready to go.

As it turns out, harnesses aren't so bad after all. They don't rub or hurt me—unlike that horrible rope my old owner would put around my neck. And even better, my harness is like a magical key to the front door. As soon as I get into it, the door opens, and I can explore the amazing world beyond.

When I went on my first walk in a big park, the outside smelled *incredible*. There was—*sniff, sniff*—cut grass and—*sniff, sniff*—pine trees and—*sniff, sniff*—my favorite smell of all—dog pee!

Freya, Mom, and I passed a tall lamppost, and I shoved my nose in a dark patch where another dog had left a little present behind for me to find. *Sniiiff!* Mom looked down at me and made a noise of revulsion. "Do you really have to put your face in that, Rolo?"

Freya laughed her chirping laugh. "I looked this up on your laptop the other night, Mom. Apparently, this is how dogs leave messages for each other. Some people call it 'pee mail!'"

Mom started laughing, too. It was the first time I'd ever heard her laugh. It was nice. Although I wasn't sure what they found so funny—we dogs need to communicate with each other somehow!

Chapter Nine
The Thunderstorm Blues

There was just one problem with living at Freya's house: every day, she left me to go to school.

In the mornings, Freya grabbed her skateboard from the shed, gave my head a pet and my ears a rub, and then she disappeared through the front door for the rest of the day.

Some mornings there would be a glimmer of hope—Freya would slam the door behind her, and then moments later, she'd come crashing back through it. She'd run to her room and grab a hat or scarf or something, but then she'd immediately rush back outside and leave me alone again. I always tried really hard to get Freya to stay. I'd lie down on her foot so she couldn't move, do sad-doggy-eyes at her, or fetch her a really good present—like a damp towel from the bathroom. But nothing ever worked.

At least Mom was at home most of the time. She'd sit at the table in the living room, in front of her laptop, and I'd curl up by her legs ready for whenever she needed a snuggle—which was becoming more and more often. She'd scratch my back, rub my tummy, and ask me that all-important question: "Who's a good boy?"

Then later in the day, after what seemed like forever, Freya would finally return home. I'd know she was coming by the crunch of feet on the driveway, the jangle of a key in the lock, and the creak of the front door opening, so I'd always rush over to greet her, sliding across the floor as if on ice.

You're home! You're home! I'd spin around in circles on my hind legs, my tail wagging crazily. "*Bark, bark, bark!*" Sometimes, I was so excited to see her that I'd pee a little on the floor. Freya would laugh. Mom wouldn't.

If there was one thing Mom *did* like, though, it was routine. When Freya didn't do the usual things at the usual times, Mom would keep repeating things like, "Freya, do your homework" and "Freya, brush your teeth." And Freya would always reply, "Later, Mom!" Freya doesn't like being told what to do. Me, neither!

And things started to fall into a routine for me, too. Every day, walks would happen at the same time, dinner would happen at the same time, trips out to the backyard to pee would happen at the same time, and bed would happen at the same time. It was completely different from my days living in the wild—back then, I never knew what was going to happen or when.

I didn't mind the routine, but I wished Mom would let me make more of my own decisions. I especially wished she'd let me choose where to sleep. If it were up to me, I'd sleep in a really cozy place, like the crook of Freya's arm in bed. But Mom won't allow me to sleep in Freya's room. She said it would get dirty, which didn't seem like a bad thing to me—dirt is wonderful! Instead, Beak Face and I had to sleep on a squishy blue mat under the radiator in the kitchen. Well, at least it was warmer than sleeping outside.

One evening, Freya carried me to my squishy mat and gave me my bedtime snuggles. After she left, I tucked Beak Face under my chin to keep him close, the way I always did. I was trying really hard to get to sleep when an awful *boom!* sounded from outside.

Thunder.

I knew the sound all too well from my days on the streets. My legs started trembling, and my teeth began chattering. I was so terrified that I got out of bed and paced back and forth, my paws going *tap tap tap* on the cold kitchen tiles.

Another clap of thunder.

I zoomed around in a panic, skidding across the floor, my paws slipping everywhere, not stopping until I banged into a chair leg.

Ow! I shook myself off. *I wish there were somewhere I could hide.... A-ha—I know!*

I waited until the thunder stopped for a moment, and then I grabbed Beak Face in my teeth, crept nervously over to one of the kitchen cupboards, and nudged the door open with my paw—the way Scrap taught me to with garbage can lids.

Inside the cupboard, there was a big box with—*sniff, sniff*—cereal inside. *Mmmm—I like cereal!* I shoved my snout deep down into the box, forgetting about the storm outside for a minute. But—*oh, no!*—now my head was stuck inside. I swished crazily back and forth, cereal flying out everywhere. I tried walking backward—or it might have been sideways—it was hard to tell when I couldn't see a thing.

It's not working! I'm going to be stuck like this forever—a dog with a box for a head! I kept shaking my head and—*oof!*—my side hit against something hard. I fell onto my bottom, and the box finally fell off my head. *Phew! That was lucky.*

I shook myself off, feeling embarrassed that I'd looked so silly in front of Beak Face. Then suddenly, the thunder sounded again, a lot closer this time, and lightning flashed through the kitchen blinds. I darted back to the cupboard to try to hide, but even without the cereal box, there still wasn't enough room for me and Beak Face.

I know—I'll make some space. I picked up a jar of pickles in my mouth, dropped it on the floor with a *thunk,* and watched it roll to the other end of the kitchen. If I wasn't so scared, I'd have loved to chase that jar!

Next, I grabbed a carton of juice and bit down hard. *Oh, all the juice is dribbling out! Oops!* After a quick slurp, I dropped the leaking carton on the floor and moved on to a box of teabags. I clamped my jaws around the box, my teeth crushing the cardboard, and the lid popped open. The teabags fell into the juice and got all soggy. The kitchen floor was a mess now, but at least there was plenty of space in the cupboard for me. I wagged my tail with satisfaction.

I was just about to clamber inside when I heard Mom's muffled voice from upstairs. "Freya—is that you clattering around?"

"No, Mom. It's probably Rolo. Don't

worry—I'll go and check on him."

Footsteps thumped down the stairs, and then Freya appeared in the kitchen doorway. "What's the matter, Rolo?" she asked. Then she saw the kitchen. "Oh, Rolo, you peed all over the floor again! Were you frightened by the storm?"

Excuse me, but I did no such thing! I thought, offended by her accusation.

"Oh, wait," she said, picking up the carton from the floor. "It's only orange juice. It looks like you've been having quite a snack. You are funny, aren't you, Rolo?" She reached down to scratch behind my ears, and I felt so glad that she was there to protect me from the storm. But then suddenly, she stopped and made a hissing sound as we both heard Mom shuffling around upstairs. "*Shhh!*"

"Freya—is everything okay down there?" Mom called from the top of the stairs.

"Y-yes! Everything's fine," said Freya, as

she looked around the kitchen in a panic. Freya and I might have thought it was funny, but Mom was sure to see things differently.

"Really? You don't sound too sure...."

"It's nothing, Mom—you go back to bed. Rolo is a little scared of the thunder, that's all. I'll get back upstairs soon, I promise."

"Well, okay, but don't be too long—you have school in the morning," Mom said as she shuffled off.

Freya grabbed a mop and started frantically wiping up the orange juice. I don't know why she didn't just lick it up— that would have been much quicker ... and tastier! Then she moved on to the rest of the mess: the cereal, teabags, and jar of pickles. I would've helped her, but I had to check if Beak Face was okay. After all, I *am* his loyal protector.

When Freya had finally finished, she

scooped me up and took me back to my mat. As she curled up next to me, I could feel the warmth of her lying behind me, and a happy feeling washed over me. "It's okay, Rolo. You're a good boy," she whispered in my ear.

I nudged her chin with my wet nose and gave her a big, sloppy kiss. *I'll never quite get used to being called a good boy*, I thought.

But Freya being there didn't mean the thunder went away, and every time it sounded, I almost jumped out of my fur.

"Aw, I wish I could sleep down here with you, Rolo, but the last time I did that, I got in trouble." Freya gave a deep sigh and rubbed my ears. "It seems like I'm always doing something wrong." Her voice sounded sad.

I gave Freya's arm a small pat with my paw as if to say, *Go on, my ears are ready and wiggling—you can tell me.*

"I don't mind Mom being mad at me, but I hate it when she scolds you. I know she doesn't mean to, but sometimes it seems like she's taking her stress out on you. That's just not fair, is it? You're only a little puppy." Freya rubbed under my chin, and then she rolled over and sprang to her feet. "A-ha—I know what'll calm you down."

Freya went to get her guitar from the living room. I liked the shiny, yellow-brown instrument. I especially liked licking the strings because they tasted really salty and a little bit greasy. But that night, I can't say I particularly liked the noise that Freya was making on it. The horrible sounds climbed higher and higher...

Twang!
Ting
Ting
Ting
Twang!

Ting

Ting

Ting

The noises sounded even worse on their way back down—like a creaky old dog, tired out from a long walk, limping and whining his way home.

"*Ow-hooowl!*" *My ears are hurting. Stop, Freya, stop!*

Freya laughed. "Poor Rolo—you don't like my playing? That's okay—practicing scales is really boring anyway because you just repeat the same notes over and over again. Let's see if I can make something up for you instead."

A beautiful noise erupted from the guitar just then. My tail started to wag along to the pretty sounds. It was like a dog on his walks again, but this time he was a young, happy pup who was full of energy. He wasn't being dragged and tugged painfully along—he got to decide where he'd like to go. He wandered here and there, sometimes jumping up high, sometimes crouching down low. Then he'd take you by surprise and run around in dizzy circles. And just when he seemed to get a little lost, he'd find his way and trot along merrily again.

Freya had a big smile on her face all the while she was playing. Her head nodded, and her yellow tail swung in time to the music. Then she turned to me and pulled gently on my ears. "I'm going to call this one *Rolo's Thunderstorm Blues*."

I leaned heavily against Freya as she continued playing, closed my eyes, and then zzz....

I was woken up by Mom's voice sometime later. It was still dark outside, but she was standing in the kitchen, looming over us.

"Freya, come on—it really is time for bed. You can't sleep down here with the dog."

"I'm sorry, Mom. I was just playing for Rolo to drown out the sound of the storm. I actually made up a pretty cool tune. Listen!" Freya's fingers crawled up and down the guitar like spiders weaving a web. She was playing the same beautiful music that she did before.

A smile spread across Mom's face, and she sank down onto the floor to sit with us. "That's beautiful, Freya. Did you really make it up all by yourself? How creative! So … what grade do you think you could get for that piece?"

What a typical Mom thing to say, I thought.

"Oh, Mom! I can't believe you asked me that!" said Freya.

Then they both burst out laughing.

Chapter Ten
That Tabby Cat

As a pet dog, I had a lot of important jobs to do. I was there to take care of Freya and make sure she was always having fun. And I was there to help Mom become more carefree, eager, excited ... more dog.

Mom seemed to spend every day working—and she worked hard. I'd heard her use the word "accountant" a bunch of times, but I didn't understand what that meant. Whatever it was, though, she sometimes seemed to forget that she had another job to do—giving me attention. What could be more important than that?

One day, I decided my mission was to allow Mom to do as little work as possible. I didn't like it when she gave her laptop all her attention and ignored me and Freya. I didn't understand why she sat indoors staring at the blue screen when we could be running around outside under the blue sky. And stopping Mom from using her machine was a great game—I could amuse myself for a long time by interrupting her. She even seemed secretly grateful to me, relieved at the excuse to stop doing her boring work.

That morning, after Freya left for school, Mom settled on the couch with her laptop at the ready. As she started clicking away, I thought, *I'll put a stop to this!* I clambered onto the cushions next to her and began to nudge her arm with my nose.

"Stop that please, Rolo. I'm trying to work." She tried to sound stern, but I could tell her heart wasn't in it when she didn't try to push me away. In fact, she looked almost sad when I started to back off—I could tell because her mouth was turned downward. So I dashed over to my mat and picked up my amazing squeaky bone toy. *Don't worry, Mom—you can play with my toy!*

I skidded back over to her and crashed into her leg. "*Squeak, squeak, squeak!*"

"Oh, Rolo! Can you be a little quieter? Just for a while?"

But I wasn't going to give in that easily. I jumped up at her leg, squeezing the toy in my mouth. "*Squeeeak!*"

"I know you want to play, Rolo, but I'm on a tight deadline."

When I kept squeezing the toy, she put down her laptop and got up from the couch.

"Rolo, give me that toy."

Yes—it's working! I took my chance and sprinted across the room with the bone in my mouth, looking behind me to check and see if Mom was following. She eventually caught up with me and tugged the toy away. It looked like she was getting the hang of playing, but I was sad the game had ended so soon. Then I had an idea— what if I swapped the squeaky yellow toy for Beak Face? He always cheered me up when I was feeling down. So I trotted to get him from my mat and scrambled back onto the couch, where Mom had returned to her work. Then I opened my mouth and dropped Beak Face onto her lap, a long thread of slobber connecting me to him.

"Rolo, you really have to stop distracting me. I can't play right now." Mom picked up Beak Face and hid him behind one of the couch cushions. "Just sit there and keep me company while I work."

I tried to win her over by doing sad-doggy-eyes, and when that failed, I squirmed my way onto her knee. She ran her hand gently along my back.

"Awww—you're cute when you're behaving yourself."

But Mom quickly returned to focusing on her screen. I heaved a sigh and slumped down onto her lap. Then the *bring-brrring* noise started.

Mom held the phone to her ear. "Good morning, Luke! Nice weekend? Now, about that report...."

Silly phone, getting all the attention! "*Bark, bark, bark!*"

"Rolo—*shhh!* Sorry about that, Luke. Could you repeat that last part? I didn't quite catch it."

"*Bark, bark, bark!*"

"I'm so sorry, Luke—"

"*Bark, bark, bark!*"

"We have a new dog, and he's a bit hyper—"

"*Bark, bark, bark!*"

"Would you mind if we rescheduled this call?"

"*Bark, bark, bark!*"

"Yes, I know our deadline's really tight, but I just can't hear you with the dog barking like crazy." Mom finally put down the phone and turned to me. She looked angry.

"Rolo! You've left me with no choice. You're going outside." She scooped me up in her hands and marched out into the backyard.

I started to whine, confused and upset by Mom's raised voice. She hesitated for a split second at the sound, the anger fading from her face. "Oh, Rolo. You'll be okay." She looked down at me sympathetically, as if she might take me back inside, but then she stepped into the kitchen without me. "It'll only be for a while so I can get some work done. Now, you have a nice run around and use up that energy of yours." With that, she closed the door firmly behind her.

She's abandoning me! I can't survive out here on my own. I'll starve or freeze or get captured by a Two Leg! I plonked my bottom down on the freezing ground and licked my fur, feeling sorry for myself. *What if Mom forgets about me and leaves me out here forever?* I sniffled.

How things had changed since my stray days. I wasn't built for the wild anymore. To be honest, I never was that good at surviving outdoors on my own. And since then, I'd become much too used to my home comforts. Too used to being a Two-Leg pet.

There wasn't much for me to do in the yard to keep my mind off sad thoughts, especially since Freya wasn't there to keep me company. No balls to chase or sticks to fetch. There was just grass, grass, and more grass. So I rolled around for a while in it. Then I got a running start and skidded through it. Then I nibbled on it. Then I dug at it. Then I ran around until I got dizzy and fell down on it.

I. Was. Bored.

I really wished Freya were back from school. She'd come out and play with me, and then let me back inside—I knew she would. I was just imagining all the fun we'd be having if she were there when….

Hey! What's that over there, sneaking around by the shed? I peered at the bottom of the shed after catching a glimpse of movement in the corner of my eye. *It's a cat!*

Now, there aren't many creatures that I dislike. But of the ones I do, cats are definitely at the top of the list. When I lived outdoors, they'd steal my food, mark my territory, or scratch me on the nose whenever I tried to play with them. They're just really, really mean.

I'm going to get you, cat. This'll keep me busy. This'll be fun!

It was that cat from next door—a tabby of gigantic proportions. I finally had the chance to chase it—and I was pretty sure I'd be able to outrun it. *Ready? Set? Doggo!*

As I closed in on the cat, it scrambled up the side of the garden shed, clinging on desperately with its claws. I gazed up at it eagerly.

"Bark, bark, bark!"

The tabby scampered across the roof, its ears flat and its tail as bushy as a fox's. I traced the line of the cat's path with my eyes from my position below, waiting for my opportunity.

"Bark, bark, bark!"

The cat took a flying leap from the roof and landed on the branch of a tree in our neighbor's yard. It was an impressive jump, I had to admit.

Hmmm…. How am I going to get over the neighbor's fence and up that tree? I was just trying to figure out my route when I was distracted by some noise coming from our house—the back door opening and then Freya's voice shouting. She must have heard me barking in the yard.

"Mom! What's Rolo doing in the backyard on his own? You know he has that condition … what did the vet call it? Separation anxiety. Why did you leave him out here by himself?"

I knew that tone all right. It signaled the start of an argument between Freya and Mom. I had to stop them. So I turned my back on the cat, who was now cowering on the highest branch of the tree, and ran to meet Freya. But just before I got to the kitchen door, I threw a final glare over my shoulder, promising the cat that I'd catch it next time.

Chapter Eleven
The Woom-Woom Sound

Freya carried me from the freezing yard back into the house. She placed me down gently on my blue squishy mat in the kitchen. Then she curled up next to me and started burrowing her fingers into my fur.

The winter sunlight spilled through the window, its pale golden rays falling onto me and Freya. I gave her a long lick on the cheek and she giggled, so I stuck my wet tongue into her ear. *Mmm—earwax!* It tasted all yummy and bitter. Mom never lets me eat her earwax. Typical. But Freya does. *Nom, nom, nom!* After my quick snack, I rolled over onto my side and Freya tickled my belly, making my back leg twitch blissfully. I felt so cozy that I could have stayed there all—

But wait! Where was Beak Face? I hadn't seen him since before Mom forced me out into the backyard. Where was he? "*Woof? Woof?*"

"Are you okay, Rolo? D'you want me to play the guitar for you? Well, you're in luck. I made up a new song last night just for you." Freya jumped up and skipped out of the kitchen, but for once I didn't want to follow her.

I could feel my heart beating faster and hear a noise in my ears going *woom-woom, woom-woom, woom-woom*. Where was my stuffed friend?

Gray clouds passed across the kitchen

window, and rain started to dribble down the glass. My head hung low, as if it were carrying the heavy weight of memories. I opened my mouth to howl, but no sound came out.

The *woom-woom* noise was getting louder and faster. I couldn't tell if it was inside my head or outside. I felt like I'd heard it before but just couldn't remember where.

I bent down and sniffed my mat—it still smelled like my friend. I breathed in the scent so deeply that it made my eyes fill with tears, so I shook my head before setting off on my hunt. *Sniff, sniff*—he's not under the table—*sniff, sniff*—or behind the garbage can—*sniff, sniff*—or stuck between the oven and the counter....

Freya came through the door just then and started to play her guitar. Usually, I'd have loved to sit and listen, and beat my tail to the tune, but not today—I *had* to find Beak Face. So I ignored her, sniffing my way around her legs, searching for any scent of my stuffed friend.

"Hey, Rolo, don't you want to listen to my guitar-playing? That's okay, boy. You just keep doing what you're doing. It looks like you're on a very important sniffing mission." Freya gave my head a kiss and left the kitchen.

Maybe Mom put him in the cupboard. I opened the closest one with my paw, and a big roll of paper towels fell out. I clenched the paper in my teeth, and a long carpet unraveled behind me. When it had all unrolled, I started chewing on the cardboard tube to calm myself down. But I knew I couldn't just sit there chomping and drooling, so I left the soggy pile of pulp in the kitchen and headed to the next room.

Mom was in there, tapping away on her laptop once again. We hadn't spoken since she'd thrown me out into the backyard.

I paused and sniffed the air suspiciously. *You know what happened to Beak Face, don't you?*

I felt like I was in pain. Not the kind of pain you get from being smacked on the bottom. I'd only ever felt this kind of pain once before—when I lost my best friend, Scrap. "*Ow-hooowl!*"

"Rolo, why are you howling like that? Calm down, little one." Mom reached over to pat me on the head. I'd usually have liked that—any attention is good attention. But no, not then.

Sniff, sniff.... *What's that?* I could smell Beak Face on Mom's hand! It was only a faint scent, but it was definitely Beak Face—I was sure of it.

I jumped up at Mom, desperately crashing my paws into her legs. "*Ruff, ruff, ruff!*" *What have you done with my friend?*

"Okay, that's enough, Rolo. You're staying in the kitchen until you stop being so excitable." Mom scooped me up off the carpet, carried me back into the kitchen, plonked me on the floor, and then left the room. I was in a panic, and I didn't know what to do. I started feeling sick and whining to myself.

The *woom-woom* noise had gotten really loud by this time. It didn't sound like it was coming from my head anymore—it sounded like it was coming from one of the kitchen machines. Then suddenly, it dawned on me. *It's the machine where dirty clothes go in and come out clean—my least favorite thing in the house!*

WOOM-WOOM, WOOM-WOOM, WOOM-WOOM. The noise hurt my head so much that it felt like it was going to burst. I darted over to the washing machine to try to make it stop. *"Ruff, ruff!"* *Stop,*

stop! You're making loud noises and hurting my ears!

I jumped up at the big round window and … I couldn't believe what I was seeing.…

Beak Face! My stuffed friend was trapped inside!

The machine was filled with foamy water that went around and around—and Beak Face was being carried around with it.

"*Ow-hooowl!*"

Mom and Freya came running into the kitchen.

"What's all this howling about, Rolo?" Mom asked.

"*Woof, woof!*" *Please, please! You have to help my friend!*

"And what happened to the paper towel roll? It's all over the floor! Rolo, what did you do that for?"

I jumped up at the machine again and again and again. I clawed frantically at the window with my front paws. I slammed my nose against the door to try to open it. I did everything I could to try to save my beloved friend.

"*Woof, woof!*"

"Mom, why is Rolo attacking the washing machine?" Freya was looking at me with a worried face. Then Beak Face pressed up against the window.

"*Woof, woof!*" *Look, Freya, look!*

"Oh, no! He can see his stuffed toy inside. He loves it—we have to get it out!"

"But you're the one who told me to wash it, Freya!"

"*Woof, woof, woof!*"

"I only said that so you wouldn't throw it in the garbage!"

"*WOOF, WOOF, WOOF!*" My friend was drowning, and I couldn't do anything!

"Please, Mom—we have to do something!"

Mom's face looked distressed as she realized just how much this meant to me. "What am I supposed to do, Freya? I can't open the door. The machine hasn't finished its cycle!"

"But I've never seen Rolo so upset! Please, Mom, please!"

Mom looked down at me, and I gazed back at her through my tears. Then she opened the machine door, and a huge cascade of foamy water came rushing out, drenching me completely. I slowly opened my stinging eyes, and there, by my paws, was a very soggy, very sorry-looking Beak Face.

Wag, wag, wag! Beak Face! You're alive! It's a miracle—I thought I'd lost you forever!

Freya clapped her hands and smiled down at me. "Look, Rolo—it's your duck friend! You've got him back!"

Sniff, sniff, sniff…. Yuck! You smell all clean

and horrible. But that's okay—the next time I go out into the backyard, I'll roll you around in the dirt. Then you'll smell all nice again!

Mom stood still and silent in the foamy pool. Her eyes got bigger and bigger as the water spread out farther and farther across the kitchen. But at least she wasn't shouting anymore.

Chapter Twelve
Cake!

Since the washing-machine episode, Mom had been doing a lot of nice little things for me. When she made dinner for herself and Freya, she gave me yummy scraps of vegetable peel. Or when she was watering the plants, she would stop by my mat to give me a kiss. She'd even started to close her laptop in the middle of working to go and chase me around the yard.

Okay, so she would still scold me sometimes, but her bark was worse than her bite. And besides, nothing would stop me from loving her now—not after she'd rescued Beak Face. I had given her my heart—just like with Freya. It felt as though Freya, Mom, and I all had these roots—like trees. And our roots had grown deep under the soil and gotten tangled up together, forever.

The only thing was, since the Big Beak Face Rescue, Mom had got even stricter than usual—probably to make sure the kitchen didn't end up flooded again. She kept trying to tell me what to do. But I didn't like being told what to do. I didn't mean any harm—I'd just gotten used to doing my own thing when I was living *rrruff*. So if Mom called me, I ran in the other direction. If she said "Stay," I'd walk away. And if she put me in the pet carrier for a long car ride, I'd bark my head off.

Mom hated it when I helped Freya make

her bed, because I'd shake the pillow wildly as if I'd caught a big fat goose. And she especially hated it when I helped Freya do the dishes. I liked doing that because just before she stacked the dirty plates in the dishwasher, Freya would let me lick them clean. *Yum!*

Hmmm, I'd really like to help Freya do the dishes now. I'd been running around in the backyard all morning, chasing the tabby cat from next door, and I was starting to miss her. *I'm going to see where she is,* I thought. I trotted into the kitchen where I could see Freya's and Mom's feet by the table—but the rest of them was lost in a cloud of white fog.

"Oh, Freya, the powdered sugar is going everywhere!"

"I'm sorry! I'm trying to measure it out, but it keeps spilling." I nudged Freya's leg to get her attention—and hopefully a bite of whatever they were making. "Awww, hello, Rolo! Have you come to help us bake a cake?"

"*Bark!*" *I've come to help you wash the dishes. Looks like you're making a lot of mess for me to lick up!*

Freya dropped a chunk of butter by my paws while Mom wasn't looking. *Schluuurp! Almost as good as my favorite treats!*

"Okay, Freya—the recipe says that we have to beat the egg whites now," Mom instructed.

Freya started tapping her foot on the floor and singing under her breath. "Beat, beat, beat the egg. You gotta beat, beat, beat the egg."

"They need to form soft peaks, like in the picture."

Freya continued the tune: "Peak, peak, peak of egg. See that peak, peak, peak of egg." I bounced around Freya's feet, jumping in time with her song. She danced, too, clapping her hands together, her yellow tail wagging up and down. Then, to my surprise, Mom joined in, spinning around with a whisk in her hand.

"Beat, beat, beat the egg. You gotta beat, beat, beat the egg," they both sang together, in between bursts of laughter.

I joined in with all the noise: "*Bark, bark, barky-bark!*"

After a while, Mom paused, took a deep breath, and said, "*Phew!* Let's get back to work—this cake won't bake itself."

They stirred and whisked, heated and cooled. Then, just as the eating was finally about to happen, there was a loud *ding-dong* at the front door.

I followed them into the hallway, where Mom opened the door to a strange Two Leg.

"I'm sorry to come over unannounced,"

said the stranger. "It's just that I need to speak to you about your dog." My ears pricked up as the stranger continued. "He's been terrorizing my cat, Queenie!" I sniffed, offended by the Two Leg's mean words. "I just heard Queenie meowing in the backyard, and when I went to look, she was stuck at the top of the tree. Your dog must have chased her up there, poor little thing!"

"Are you sure it was Rolo?" said Mom. "I mean—did you actually see him chasing the cat or…."

"I'm positive—I saw him jumping up at the fence trying to get Queenie just last week. She was terrified! She wouldn't go outside for days afterward! And now that she's gotten up the courage again, he's scared her silly!"

Freya crouched down to where I was sitting on the hallway rug. She gave me a gentle tickle under the ear, which made me feel a bit better about being so unfairly blamed—this Two Leg clearly hadn't thought about my side of the story.

Freya gave me a little wink and then turned back to the Two Leg. "I'm so sorry, Mrs. Brennan, I really am. Rolo's my puppy, so it's all my fault."

"Well, it looks like Rolo could use some training."

Training? What would I need training for? I'm the best-behaved dog around.

"I've been trying to train him, I really have, but it's harder than I thought. He was living on the streets when we found him and took him in."

"Well, I suppose that explains it." Mrs. Brennan's face softened a little.

"We really are sorry," Mom added. "If you aren't in a rush, Freya and I just baked a cake—why don't you stay and join us for a piece?"

"Oh … if you're sure. That would be nice! Thank you."

Freya led Mrs. Brennan into the living room, and I trotted behind them.

"I spoke to your mom over the fence last week, Freya—she told me you play guitar," Mrs. Brennan said, taking a seat by the coffee table. "She said you're getting pretty good. I hear you've even started composing your own pieces. That's very impressive!"

Freya's cheeks flushed, and I could tell she was secretly happy that Mom had been telling people about her songs. "Oh, they're just for fun, really. They're not very good."

"Well, that's not what your mom said."

"Um, thanks. One day, when I'm older, I want to be in a band." Freya's face was full of smiles as they continued talking.

A few minutes later, Mom entered the room and placed a plate on the coffee table with the cake on it. It smelled like the things that were in the kitchen, but all mixed up into one delicious doggy snack! My tail started to wag against the carpet, and dribble ran down my chin. I licked my lips at the thought of it.

Let's see.... Mom and Freya haven't called out "dinner," but they put the cake on the table where I can reach it. And I know I'm not allowed to jump up at the table, but the cake looks so yummy and sticky and.... Oh, I just can't wait any longer!

Quick as anything, I stood up on my hind legs, slammed my front paws on the table, and snapped my jaws around the cake.

"No, Rolo, no!" Mom shrieked. She dove at the plate, Freya dove at me, and the other Two Leg dove out of the way. The plate wobbled across the table and landed on the floor, smashing into pieces and spraying yellow crumbs all over the carpet.

A cake shower! How exciting! "Bark, bark, bark!" I cheered as I vacuumed up the mess with my mouth.

I noticed Freya biting her lip, trying not to laugh—but Mom took a big gulp, as if she were swallowing a mouthful of angry words. "I'm so sorry, Mrs. Brennan. This is so embarrassing! I didn't see him under the coffee table and…."

"It's fine. These things happen. Look, I think I'd better go and leave you in peace. We can always do this another afternoon." The Two Leg started to walk toward the front door. "Oh, before I go…. Let me give you the number of an excellent trainer I know. She runs obedience classes for dogs not far from here."

Mom took out her phone and started tapping away at it frantically. She was up to something, I could tell. And while I didn't know what obedience meant, I was pretty sure it wasn't going to be anything good….

Chapter Thirteen
Doggy School

Sometimes it's hard being so small. When I go for my walks in the park, it seems like every strange Two Leg who sees me wants to fuss over me and pick me up. And that's really scary, because they're always so big. So I might growl or bark. I don't mean to be unfriendly—it's just my way of saying, *"Please don't do that! I'm scared."*

If only Two Legs learned how to speak Dog.... But I don't think there's any such thing as a school where Two Legs can learn

Dog. Instead, *I* was the one who had to go to school and learn how to behave myself. I loved Freya and Mom, and I would've done anything to make them happy. Anything except behaving myself.

When we arrived, we were all introduced to the teacher—a soft-spoken young female named Ms. Abara. She seemed—and smelled—nice enough, but I was still suspicious of what she was going to do. Mom, however, immediately went over to her and started bombarding her with questions. "How will the training work exactly? What if he doesn't get along with the other dogs? How long will it all take?"

After she'd explained everything to Mom, Ms. Abara called everyone together and led us to a big, grassy field. I was a little nervous, because all of the other dogs seemed to know what was happening. They'd clearly been to classes before.

Ms. Abara introduced me, Freya, and Mom, and then after an awkward pause, a large female Alsatian barked in a deep voice, "Welcome to the pack, Rolo!"

She must be the alpha female, I thought, because the other dogs promptly started copying her and barking friendly things at me.

"Hello, there!"

"Great to meet you!"

"Let's be friends!"

But my attention was soon diverted from my new friends to Ms. Abara, who was waving something in the air.

"Good," she said as we all fell silent to stare eagerly at the toy in her hand. "Now, as we have some newcomers today, let me just summarize what Think Pawsitive is all about. Essentially, this course is about training young puppies who are particularly challenging. And the really important thing is that we're committed to ensuring you only learn positive training techniques. So I want you to forget anything you might've heard about dog training before. And from now on, you'll learn how to avoid the use of pain, fear, and intimidation at all times.

"Let's take our new boy, Rolo, as an example. Rolo used to be a stray, so he hasn't been socialized yet. Now, let's see what could happen if a stranger like me approaches him too quickly...."

Eek! There's a big hand coming toward my face! I'd better bite it in case it's up to no good. Naughty hand—take that! I went to snap my teeth around the Two Leg's fingers.

"As you can see, unsocialized puppies tend to bite. Luckily for me, I've got these strong leather gloves on. But we can't just hand out pairs of super-thick gloves to anyone who might come in contact with our puppies, can we? So what *can* we do about it?"

Mom raised her hand and said, "Should we say 'No!' in a stern voice?"

"That's a really good guess, but we need to be careful. If we try to dominate our dog, the confrontation will actually *encourage* them to be aggressive. Remember — we want to maintain the positive, loving bond that we've built up with them. Any more suggestions?"

"Um, could we … use some kind of nice treat, like food or something?" Freya said shyly.

"Excellent, Freya!" Ms. Abara said with a smile. "We can encourage good behavior in our dogs by using rewards like food, toys, and petting. For example, we can use a technique called Touch and Treat. Freya— can you please give Rolo a nice pet?"

Ooh! Freya's hand feels wonderful on my back!

"And next, we give Rolo a treat...."

A treat! Nom, nom, nom.

"Look—see how his aggression seems to be disappearing?"

Wag, wag, wag. This is great! I love getting attention and being petted. And even better, delicious dog treats are just appearing out of the air. If this is what Doggy School is going to be like, I can definitely get on board.

The following Saturday, it was time for me to go back to school. The other dogs had already arrived on the grassy field with their owners by the time we got there. They all kept a close eye on the she-Alsatian, and when she pricked up her ears to listen to the teacher, they all copied.

"Now, some puppies have a really hard time giving up objects like toys and food,"

Ms. Abara said. "They can guard things obsessively. Sound familiar, anyone?" She looked around the group of Two Legs, who all smiled knowingly.

"Well, if we're not careful, this behavior can turn into a real issue. But the good news is, there's a solution: the Take It, Drop It technique. This is a great way of getting puppies to drop things when we need them to."

Ms. Abara started to hand out some objects to the Two Legs. Then everyone spread out to find a spot on the field.

Freya and Mom walked me over to a quiet space away from the others. Then Freya held up the toy she'd been given and shook it in front of me.

A stuffed mouse! Come here, mousey! You're mine! I leaped into the air, trying desperately to snatch the stuffed toy.

"What's this, Rolo?" she said, moving it

closer to my nose. "Take it!"

I grabbed hold of the mouse between my teeth.

"Yes. Good boy!" Freya clapped. I bounced around the grass, delighted with my prize.

But wait—hang on. What does Freya have in her hand now? It's another stuffed mouse! I trotted back over to investigate.

Freya shook the mouse at me.

Hmmm. What if Freya's new mouse is even better than this one?

She dangled the new mouse right in front of my nose. I bit down on it hard and was just enjoying chewing on it when I realized that something was wrong.

Hey—what happened to my old mouse? It's been taken away!

After a pause, Freya put the old mouse back under my nose again. I grabbed it in my mouth, and the game continued. I dropped the mouse, I got a new mouse, I dropped that mouse, I got a new mouse....

I looked around the field at the other dogs. They were all doing toy droppings and grabbings, too. It felt good to be part of the pack.

Ms. Abara spoke to the class in a loud voice: "When your puppy starts to think of giving up the toy as a game, then there's no need to guard it from people. It all becomes part of the fun."

As Freya played with me, she bounded around the grass saying, "Drop it. Take it. Good! Drop it. Take it. Good!"

Mom was running around with us, too, a big smile on her face. "That's it, Rolo! Great job, Freya! Excellent work—keep it up!"

Every now and then, Mom would stop to greet the other owners and pet their dogs. "Hi there—what a beautiful puppy you have…. Your dog is so well behaved! Very impressive…. What breed is yours? A cockerpoo? How adorable!"

By the time spring arrived, I'd been to Doggy School a bunch of times. (I can't say exactly how many, though, because I can only count to four!) Just before the latest class was about to start, I heard Mom talking to Ms. Abara as she always did before and after our lessons.

"… I knew there had to be more to life than sitting at a desk, never seeing the blue sky or breathing the fresh air," Ms. Abara was saying. "So I just handed in my notice one day and started my dog-training business the next."

"Good for you!" said Mom. "Sometimes I dream about doing that kind of thing.

That is, if I have any time left to dream after I've finished work for the day!"

"Mom, have you ever thought about looking for a new job?" Freya joined in. "You don't seem to like your current one very much. You're always saying how much it stresses you out."

Mom looked at Freya, then down at me, and said in a slow voice, "Sometimes."

We wandered over to the other dogs and their Two Legs, where Mom spent a lot of time petting them all. She petted the she-Alsatian who, I must confess, even I was a little scared of. Then she started asking Ms. Abara really detailed questions, using words I didn't understand, like "career," "insurance," and "qualifications."

It was a good lesson, because Ms. Abara spent extra time with me, Mom, and Freya, giving me in particular a lot of attention.

"Now, I know Rolo doesn't like cats, so

I'm going to show him a big photo of a cat and see what he does," Ms. Abara explained to Mom and Freya. "The idea is for him to learn not to bark so much. But we have to take it step by step. So at first, we're not going to do anything if he barks at the cat."

Ms. Abara placed a stand next to me on the grass with a pad of white paper attached to it. Then she lifted up a flap of paper and revealed … a huge, horrible gray cat!

"*Woof, woof, woof!*" I jumped up at the big stand again and again until I knocked it onto the grass. *Take that, evil cat!*

Ms. Abara picked up the stand. "Okay, now let's try distracting him. Freya—try using this toy ball. See if it'll stop him from barking."

But I wasn't interested in the ball. The cat had reappeared above my head! "*Woof, woof, woof!*"

"I don't understand why it's not working— he usually loves playing ball with me," said

Freya, although I was only half listening.

"Don't worry. Let's try something else. Now, whenever Rolo barks, I'd like us to walk away from him. We're not going to go far—just up to that bench."

"Woof, woof, wo—" Hey, wait! Where's everyone going?

I darted over to the bench where Freya and the others were standing.

"Just keep ignoring him when he barks. We're not being mean—it's for his own good."

What's going on? Why are you ignoring me? "Woof, woof, woof!"

"When he's quiet, we can go back over to the cat photo."

"Come on, Rolo—you can do this. Be a good boy," Mom said.

Mom's encouraging words gave me a warm feeling in my tummy. I fell silent for a few seconds.

"Look—Rolo isn't barking anymore!"

Freya said. "Should we go back to the picture now?"

Ms. Abara nodded, and they all began to walk back to where we'd started, slowly, cautiously. And I followed along, until....

"*Woof, woof, woof!*" *Look—there's that horrible cat again!* I thought, looking at the photo. But my woofs had sent everyone away again. So I fell quiet and followed them.

We went backward and forward, from the bench to the cat to the bench again, until I grew bored of woofing. It was just a silly photo of a cat, after all. And, well, I was no detective dog, but I did get the feeling that if I kept on woofing, everyone would walk away from me again.

As we approached the cat the last time, I could hear Freya and Mom holding their breath as they waited to see what I'd do. But even though the mean gray furball seemed to be glaring at me, I avoided the temptation.

I stayed completely silent.

"Yay! It worked, it worked, it worked!" Freya yelled at the top of her voice. Then Mom and Ms. Abara joined in, cheering away. I didn't understand what all the fuss was about, but I joined in with the celebrations anyway.

Ms. Abara struggled to get her breath back. "Great work, you two! Give him a dog treat, quickly. Reward him for his good behavior."

Crouching down, Mom spoke into my ear. "I can't believe you did it! You really did it! Good boy. I'm so proud of you." She handed me a treat, and I gobbled it up eagerly.

Then Mom grabbed Freya and Ms. Abara by their hands. They danced around and around in a circle, with me running in and out of their feet, and Mom laughing the loudest out of everyone.

At last—I'd finally trained Mom to have some fun!

Chapter Fourteen
Bad Boy

We were one big, happy pack: me, Freya, Mom, and Beak Face. (Well, except when I destroyed the odd slipper or muddied one of the carpets—that still made Mom unhappy.) Although I'd only lived in the house for a few months, I really think they needed me as much as I needed them.

When Mom was tense and cranky from a hard day's work, I could smell the stress all over her. So I'd bound over, do sad-doggy-eyes, and lure her out into the backyard to play ball, and she'd forget all about her worries.

When Freya was working at her desk, staring at her books and looking bored, I'd carefully remove a sock from her foot, just to let her know I was there for her. Or when she was in need of a hug, Beak Face and I would come to her rescue. And she was as loyal to me as I was to her—she'd never forget to give me my daily meals and weekly baths. Mom always seemed to be very impressed with that. Almost every day, she'd call Freya a good girl and me a good boy.

Most important of all, we loved going on walks together—especially on the weekend. I'd finally grasped the bizarre Two-Leg concept of weekends. See, they split the week into these different chunks. They dedicate the biggest chunk to the boring, serious stuff: doing their work or going to school, leaving only a small chunk at the end of the week for all the fun stuff. Strange! I just couldn't understand why they didn't spend all their time playing and doing whatever they liked.

Anyway, on one of these weekends, we headed off to my all-time favorite place— the woods! I could tell that was where we were going because Freya and Mom both had their blue rain boots on. The woods were far away from home, so we didn't go very often. This was a real treat, and I just couldn't wait. *Wag, wag, wag!*

As soon as we got there, I saw a fat, fuzzy squirrel looking for acorns in the brown and yellow leaves. *Ready or not, squirrel, here I come!* I crept forward, crouching as low as I could. Every few steps I stopped, lifted my front paw, and sniffed the air— just like Scrap used to do when she hunted squirrels. Then, as soon as the creature wasn't looking, I raced across the ground in bounding leaps: *chaaarge!* My ears flapped behind me, my paws pounded the path, and I was a whisker away from the squirrel when....

"Here, Rolo! Come here, and I'll give you a treat!" Freya was calling me back to her.

Hmmm. Squirrel or treat? That's an easy choice. I obeyed Freya and ran right back to her side. Whatever that squirrel tasted like, it couldn't possibly be as delicious as a treat.

"Good boy, Rolo. I think the squirrels are safe from you for now," Freya laughed.

Together, we headed into the woods. Then when we were surrounded by trees, Mom crouched down to let me off my harness. *Hooray! Freedom!*

Freya and I ran along together, flying through the leaves, splashing in the puddles, splattering mud into the air, and Mom calling after us, "Faster, faster!"

And then came the *bring-brrring, bring-brrring, bring-brrring*.

"Oh, Mom, do you have to answer work calls now?"

Mom glanced at Freya but lifted the phone to her ear anyway. "Mr. Swan! Wonderful to hear from you."

Freya grumbled something under her breath, something too quiet for even me to hear, and stomped off in a huff. I was just about to follow her when I overhead Mom saying my name.

"I think your Milo will get along really well with my Rolo. He loves making friends with new dogs…. Great—I'll come over and pick him up first thing in the morning."

"*Bark?*" *A new dog to make friends with? Tomorrow? Wag, wag, wag….*

Mom ended the call, rushed to catch up with Freya, and then said, "I'm really sorry, sweetheart—that was important."

"It's always important," Freya sulked.

"This time it really is—I promise. I'm making a big change tomorrow: for you, me, Rolo—for all of us. You'll see...."

I could sense that Freya was still upset despite what Mom said, so I bounded along the muddy path, flew through the air, and landed with a *splat* in the middle of a huge pile of leaves. I rolled and thrashed and growled and chased my tail, not stopping until Freya burst out laughing. Just like me, she never stays sad for long.

Soon, we reached a shady path with prickly hedges on either side. The rocky ground hurt my soft paw pads. I didn't like that part of the woods, but I kept following Freya and Mom like the good boy I was, knowing it was only a short stretch of path until we got out into the open again.

Up ahead in the distance, a big Two Leg suddenly appeared out of nowhere. It wore a long coat, its eyes were hidden behind dark glasses, its hair was poking out of a hat, and....

Oh, no....

It can't be....

It looks just like ... my old owner!

He was the same height, with the same gray hair and the same hunched walk. As he got closer, I felt my fur prickle all over and my stomach lurch. I froze, not knowing what to do. My instinct was to turn and run, but I had to stay to protect Freya and Mom from him!

"Come on, Rolo—you can't stop here." Mom didn't sound scared—but then she didn't know what my old owner was capable of.

I have to frighten him away before he hurts Freya or Mom. I'm the only one who can save them! So ignoring all my instincts, I charged right at the Two Leg, growling and barking. "*Grrruff, ruff, ruff!*"

But he kept walking toward us. "He's a feisty little one, isn't he?"

"I'm so sorry—I don't know what's come over him!" said Mom. "He never behaves like this anymore."

The evil Two Leg was now only a short distance from Mom and Freya. *Gulp! I have to be brave. I have to do something!*

I rose up on my hind legs and crashed into him with my muddy paws, growling as loudly and fiercely as I could. "*GRRRUFF, RUFF, RUFF!*"

But the Two Leg just brushed himself off and kept on walking right past us. And as he did, I caught his scent. It was completely different from my old owner's, who smelled like cigarette smoke and shoe polish. Which meant ... this wasn't him at all. It was just a normal Two Leg....

As I started to realize my mistake, Mom

began shouting at me in a stern voice that she hadn't used in a long time. "Rolo! Don't growl at people like that! No! *Bad boy!*"

Freya joined in, too. "Rolo, you can't behave like that. It's not nice."

I was so upset to see them angry that I made a run for it, darting back down the shady path and deep into the woods. When I finally stopped running, I tried to get my muddled thoughts into some kind of order.

I didn't mean to growl at a stranger. I made a mistake—I was scared. I was only trying to protect Freya and Mom!

Then I gazed around at my new surroundings. It was spookily quiet. Freya and Mom would usually come after me if I ran too far away. Where were they? I knew I was the one who'd left them, but I wanted them to find me and take me back. Then I remembered Mom's sharp, angry voice. *She called me a bad boy. My old owner used to call me that because he didn't love me. Maybe Mom doesn't love me anymore, either. I guess she'll never come back for me now.*

The bleak words circled my head like dark ravens: *bad boy, bad boy, bad boy....*

I sank down onto my paws and rested my head on the ground. *Maybe I really am a bad boy—maybe I'm better off alone. I only end up disappointing everyone. Maybe I should stay in the woods and fend for myself. I survived before—I can do it again.*

Tears started to well up in my eyes at the mere thought. *But what about Freya? She's my best friend! I'd run alongside her skateboard to the ends of the Earth.* I was a pet through and through now—I belonged to a family, and losing them was a punishment worse than a life outdoors in the cold.

I was so distressed that I couldn't bring myself to move, so I just sat there in the undergrowth, shivering for what felt like hours. The wind ruffled my fur like an icy hand rubbing my fur the wrong way. The leaves on the trees changed from yellow to gray as the evening shadows loomed. I was all alone. And I was scared.

My thoughts became as dark as the night sky. *What have I done? How am I going to survive on my own? Maybe I could go back to Freya and Mom…. But even if I do manage to find my way home, they might be so angry that they turn me away.* I knew the pain of such a rejection would be too much—enough to break my heart.

But Freya and Mom aren't cruel like my old owner. They're different. They're the only real family I've ever had. This hopeful thought quickly vanished as I realized just how much my bad behavior had cost me. I let out a howl—the biggest of my life. "*OW-HOOOWL!*"

When the sound had stopped ringing in

my ears, I expected to hear nothing, just silence, but then my ears pricked up as I heard voices in the distance. I couldn't help myself from going to check—I set off at a sprint, heading right for the noise. But as I got closer, the nagging doubt in my head sounded again—they'd never come for me, never love me again, after what I'd done—would they?

I clambered into a prickly bush to pull myself together.

And then I heard the voice I knew better than any other.

"What are we going to do, Mom? We've looked everywhere!" It was Freya.

"I don't know, sweetheart. I just don't know." Mom sounded miserable.

Peering out through the leaves, I could see Freya's shoulders shaking and her face crinkling up.

Tears started to trickle down Freya's

cheeks—and then Mom started to cry, too. "I'm so sorry, honey. I can't believe Rolo is gone. I miss him already."

What? They're crying over me? I couldn't believe what I was hearing. *Maybe I was wrong. Maybe they do still love me after all.*

I slowly crept out of the bush and gave a small, tentative whine.

Freya was the first to see me.

"Rolo!" Her face broke into the biggest smile I'd ever seen, and she came running toward me. "We found you! Oh, thank goodness! I thought we'd lost you forever! We've been looking for you for hours!"

Mom scooped me up off the ground and buried her face deep in my fur. "I'm so sorry for shouting at you, Rolo. I know you must have been scared. I was wrong." Then she nuzzled me to her chest and said, "I love you, Rolo."

Chapter Fifteen
Together Again

The next day, it was still the weekend, so we all went out for a walk again. But the vehicle we got into wasn't the one Mom usually drove. Instead, a Two Leg had knocked at the door early that morning to drop off a new van—one that looked really dog-friendly. Mom put me in the back part, where there were soft blankets everywhere, brightly colored dog toys, a textured mat to search for yummy treats in, and a ton of space for me to roll around. *Why is there so*

much space when there's only me in the back? You could fit a bunch of dogs in here!

Freya started asking questions, too. "What's with the new van, Mom? Where are we going? Why do we have to leave so early? Can't you just tell us what's happening?"

But all Mom would say was, "It's a surprise."

Soon, we came to a stop outside a house I didn't recognize. From inside the van, I heard Mom walk up a gravel path and ring a doorbell.

I rose up on my hind legs to try to look out of the window to see what was going on, but the new van was so huge that I couldn't get anywhere near the glass. Then I tried jumping on the seats—*boing, boing, boing!*—but they were so springy that I kept falling back onto my bottom. Freya was too busy staring out of her own window to help me.

"I'll bring him back in two hours. Then we can discuss a schedule going forward," I heard Mom saying to someone—but I couldn't see who.

"What on Earth is going on?" Freya mumbled from the front seat.

As Mom walked back to the van, I could smell—*sniff, sniff*—a very strong scent of dog. Then the back door of the van swung open and in jumped a dog I'd never seen before!

Mom, who had gotten back into the front seat, looked at me with a huge smile on her face and said, "Rolo—meet Milo. He's going to be your new walking buddy."

Ah! I remember! And suddenly the conversation I'd heard Mom having on the phone in the woods yesterday came back to me. In the drama of the day, I'd forgotten all about it!

Milo was just a little smaller than me, with

big blue eyes and a white coat patterned with dark spots. I sniffed at him to check him out. His body looked relaxed, his tail was wagging, and his mouth was closed and turned up slightly at the corners. He looked nice and friendly, like he'd be a lot of fun to play with.

"Hi! My name is Rolo!" I barked.

"Hi, Rolo! I'm Milo!"

"I like your spotted coat—I've never seen a dog with a coat like yours before!"

"Thanks! It's been spotted like this ever since I was a few dog weeks old."

"We're going on our walks now—do you like walks?"

"I *love* walks!" Milo's tail started to thump against the van door. "But … I haven't been able to go very often lately. My owner's getting old and has trouble walking. I've really missed running around with him." Milo's face became sad.

"Don't worry—it'll be okay," I said. "My owners are the nicest Two Legs ever. Their names are Mom and Freya, and they'll take care of you like you're their own pet dog. And I'll take good care of you, too. I've always wanted a doggy playmate! I just know we're going to be the best of friends!"

To show Milo that I truly wanted to be his friend, I offered up my snout to him. He leaned forward slowly and gave me a big, sloppy lick on my nose. *I think he likes me, too!* I chuckled to myself.

Meanwhile, Freya and Mom were deep in conversation about something important-sounding. I was only listening with one ear, though, because I was too busy with my new playmate.

"I had no idea you were planning such a big change, Mom."

"Well, it might seem sudden, but I've always wanted to start my own business.

Be my own boss, have my own restaurant, run my own llama farm…. Well, maybe a llama farm wouldn't be very practical!"

Freya started to giggle. "I'm so happy you gave up your old job! It made you so miserable."

"Thanks, sweetheart. I know. And now I'll be able to spend every day doing something I've really grown to love."

"Does that mean what I think it means? That you love dogs as much I do now?"

Then Mom started laughing, too. "Freya—no one in the entire world loves dogs as much as you do!"

Milo and I raced around the park, exploring every corner of it together. We sniffed at lampposts, pieces of litter, and each other's bottoms; we charged at the birds and the squirrels; we chased after Freya as she sped down the paths on her skateboard. We were having the best time ever. After a while, I even let Milo carry Beak Face in his mouth!

As we zoomed around the grass, Mom stayed close behind, stopping every now and then to pick up our poop. Mom is obsessed with my poop, so much so that she carries around these poop-collecting bags just in case I ever leave some behind. And then she pounces on it like it's an amazing stick to play with! I can understand why, though—I love poop as much as she does. So when Milo did one while we were out on our walks, I ran right up to it, took a good sniff, and then rolled around in it. It was wonderful!

"Rolo! Milo! Come here, doggies!" It was Mom. I recognized her tone at once —she wanted us to come quickly. As we bounded over, she turned to Freya. "Human alert!

You keep a close eye on Rolo, okay? I'll watch Milo."

I whipped my head around to where Mom was pointing. In the distance, I could make out the shape of a Two Leg appearing over the hill. *Gulp*. A nervous feeling started to bubble up in my tummy. I was fine with Two Legs that I already knew, like Freya, Mom, and the mail carrier—but I was probably always going to be unsure about ones I'd never met before. I turned to Milo to see if he was scared, but he was as calm as a summer day.

The Two Leg was getting really close to us now. But I knew that if I didn't woof, Freya would give me a treat as a reward. So even though I was scared, I stayed as quiet as I could.

Freya reached into her pocket, just like she'd been trained to do, and pulled out some yummy treats. She dropped them on the ground for me and Milo.

Good girl! Nom, nom, nom!

The stranger crouched down and gave Milo a gentle pat on the head. His tail started to spin around like crazy. He actually seemed to enjoy it!

As the Two Leg moved its hand closer to me, Mom said, "Oh, um, I'm not sure about Rolo. He's a little nervous around people he doesn't know."

"Oh, it's okay, Mom—let the lady try. Rolo has to learn—and he won't bite or anything."

I looked at Freya. She smiled.

The strange hand got closer.

I looked at Mom. She nodded.

The hand came even closer.

I looked at Milo. He panted encouragingly.

Well, maybe I could let the stranger give me a quick pat on the head. A warm hand gently landed on top of my cold head before I had time to think twice. As it moved slowly backward toward my neck, a pleasant tingle rippled through me.

Oh, that feels nice!

"He's beautiful! You're lucky to have him," the Two Leg said as she stood up and headed off.

Mom looked at me with a small smile and said, "Yes—yes, we are."

And then away we went in the other direction. I could tell we were coming to the end of our walk now because Freya clipped my leash back onto my harness. It was a shame, because we were coming to the best place in the entire park: the muddy pond!

As we approached, I started tugging on my leash, desperate to go and splash around in the muck. Freya slowed down and looked at Mom. "Should we?"

"Oh, sure—let them go wild!" They both

crouched down. Mom unclipped Milo. *Click!* Freya unclipped me. *Click!* And then there was no stopping us.

Milo and I dashed for the water, crashed into the brown pond, and sank under the ripples. A moment later we reappeared, with muddy water in our eyes and grinning mouths. I paddled over to Milo and lunged at him. We both went down under the water again, our legs kicking in slow motion under the surface. Then we popped back up, tails swishing and mouths wide open, panting with pure joy.

When we started to get tired, we headed back to the grassy bank where Mom and Freya were watching us from a bench. As soon as we reached them, we shook our wet fur wildly, sending a spray of muddy water flying all over them. They cried out together and collapsed into laughter. Then Milo and I curled up beside their warm legs to get dry again.

Wag, wag, wag. This is great! I'm lying outside in the warm sun next to my best friends—and I'm making a new friend, too! Life doesn't get much better than this.

Freya and Mom watched the fluffy white clouds drift slowly across the bright blue sky. Every now and then, they'd point upward and shout, "That one looks like a sock!" or "That one looks like a bone!" or "That one looks like a cat!"

"Are you having a nice time, Freya?"

"Of course! I always love walks with Rolo. And having two of them is double the fun!"

"Good—because we'll be taking out a lot more dogs besides Milo."

"I know—I'm so excited!" Freya turned to face her. "And Mom … now that you'll be walking dogs all the time, things could get pretty hectic. Sooo … maybe I should miss a day of school every now and then, just to help you take care of all of them."

"Nice try, Freya!" Mom raised her eyebrows and smiled. "You're not getting out of school. But I'd love for you to help me every weekend. Who's going to scoop all that poop otherwise?"

Once Milo and I had rinsed off in a clean stream, it was time to head back to the van. A deep-gold sun was sitting low in the sky, and as the four of us walked together, our shadows grew long as though having a well-deserved stretch after such a busy afternoon.

The air filled with a sunset chorus of birdsong. Freya started to join in, whistling a quiet tune of her own. Then Mom whistled a pretty harmony over the top. By now, I'd learned that Two Legs whistle like that when they're feeling happy.

Suddenly, something distracted me. I caught the whiff of a particular smell. It was just a wisp on the breeze, but it was definitely familiar to my sensitive nose. I looked up to where the smell was coming from. In the distance, I could see a pair of silhouettes: a Two Leg, and walking calmly by his side, a dog. A dog with long, long beagle ears….

No, it can't be… I thought as I strained to see so far away. *It is! It's her!*

My heartbeat sounded loudly in ears. My nose started to sniffle, and a tear fell from my eye, landing at my paws. I'd missed my old friend so, so much!

But who was that stranger walking her? She seemed to be trotting alongside him perfectly willingly. He must be her owner—why else would she seem so comfortable with him? So it appeared that even the wildest dog needed a Two Leg to call her own.

I saw my friend turn her head my way—

she must have caught my scent, too! I wanted to bark, to tell her I was okay, that I wasn't alone anymore, that I was loved. But I knew she'd never hear me from so far away.

I lurched forward on my harness, but it felt like I might pull Freya's arm out of its socket, so I held back. My friend lurched forward on her leash, too, but her owner started to guide her away.

Freya and Mom continued in the direction of the van, completely unaware of what was happening. But I wasn't ready to give up—so I lay down on the path and made myself as heavy as possible.

Freya stopped abruptly. "Mom—something's up with Rolo. I think he wants to be let off his leash."

It was working! I gazed up at Freya and let out a pleading whine. Then I pointed myself in my friend's direction, staring at her longingly.

"He seems to want to approach that dog." Freya said, pointing to my friend. "Can he, Mom? Just for a minute? He seems so determined."

Mom nodded. "Okay, just for a minute."

Freya unclipped my harness. "Go, Rolo, go!"

I was free! I was off my leash! I bolted like a greyhound from a starting box.

"Bark, bark, bark!" Wait! Wait for me! I'm coming for you, Scrap!